Dear Reader,

Do you ever watch the news? I wouldn't recommend it. I usually come away from my daily dose feeling sad and anxious. Except for when they do something about a dog that can breakdance or a stoat that predicts the outcomes of football matches. That's always a delight.

But watching bad things happen around the world can make you feel powerless, like there's too much darkness for you to do anything about it. Well, I'm here to tell you, dear reader, that that is wrong. You see, you can make a difference. It doesn't have to be something huge. It can be something as simple as telling someone you like their shoes, or lending them that book you think they'll love. And when you do nice things for people, it makes you feel good, doesn't it? And that makes you want to do more nice things so you can keep that good feeling going. And that person you've done the nice thing for? They're more likely to do a nice thing for someone else. Then, little by little, your world gets a wee bit nicer.

That's what this book is about, at least in part. It's about making a difference in whatever small way you can. It's about being as kind as you can and it's about seeking that feeling, the one you get when you know you've done a good thing, that's as warm and satisfying as a bowl of delicious soup.

Thanks for reading!

In Memory of Nanny Betty

OXFORD
UNIVERSITY PRESS

Great Clarendon Street, Oxford OX2 6DP

Oxford University Press is a department of the University of Oxford.
It furthers the University's objective of excellence in research, scholarship,
and education by publishing worldwide. Oxford is a registered trade mark of
Oxford University Press in the UK and in certain other countries

Text copyright © Ben Davis 2020
Illustrations copyright © Julia Christians 2020

The moral rights of the author have been asserted

First published 2020

Database right Oxford University Press (maker)

British Library Cataloguing in Publication Data
Data available

ISBN: 978-0-19-274923-9

3 5 7 9 10 8 6 4 2

Printed in India by Manipal Technologies Limited

Paper used in the production of this book is a natural,
recyclable product made from wood grown in sustainable forests.
The manufacturing process conforms to the environmental
regulations of the country of origin.

This story was inspired by the work
of Richard Brabin, who started a real-life
'Soup Movement' by delivering soup to the
homeless people of Oxford on the
back of his bike.

THE
SOUP
MOVEMENT

BEN DAVIS

OXFORD
UNIVERSITY PRESS

So we grew together,

Like to a double cherry, seeming parted,

But yet an union in partition,

Two lovely berries moulded on one stem.

—William Shakespeare
A Midsummer Night's Dream

CHAPTER
1

I shield my eyes from the sun and look up at the tree.
The cat is well and truly stuck. I saw next door's dog
chase it up there and now it can't get back down. I
can hear it meowing and moaning. Ugh. I'm going to
have to get it down, aren't I?

I don't want to. I'm not that keen on cats and I'm
definitely not keen on heights. But I kind of have no
choice. It's complicated.

I take one last look around the cul-de-sac to see
if anyone else is coming to help, but it's deserted.
After a lifetime in the city, the quiet is eerie. We've
been living here in Pondstead for about six months.
Mum reckons the air is cleaner. I don't know, maybe
it is. And it's nice and calm, and there's a field behind
our house where people ride horses, but Pondstead
is also kind of dull.

I dry my forehead with the back of my hand.

It's hot today. Occasionally, a cool breeze drifts across the field, but the effect is cancelled out by the fact that it's wafting horse poo.

I get a foothold and hoist myself onto the first branch. Man, this tree is huge, easily as tall as our house. I squint through the blinding light and plot my route up. I've never been much of a tree climber. Ross, my best mate, back in the city, was really good at tree climbing. If he was here, the cat would be down in no time.

I shakily stand and pull myself onto the next branch. 'Here, kitty,' I say. 'Come on down, eh? Do your old mate Jordan a favour.'

The cat looks down at me like I'm coming to strangle it. Nevertheless, I have to keep going. I shuffle along to the trunk and reach across to the other side to get to the next branch. I'm pretty high up now. I can see into my bedroom. When I look down, my stomach lurches.

Slowly, I make my way upwards, until I'm sitting on the branch on the other side of the trunk to the cat. I've seen it around before. The other day, I scared it off when I saw it about to pounce on a blackbird. I reach across to try and pet it.

RRAAAOOWW!

Ow! The horrible thing has just scratched my hand. I'm bleeding!

'What's the matter with you? I'm trying to help!'

The cat glowers at me like it's going to go for my throat next.

'Look,' I say, trying to use my most calming voice. 'I know you're scared. I am, too. But if you let me help you, I'll get you down safely and you can murder as many birds as you like.'

Hmm. Maybe that worked. Its back isn't all arched like it was before. Time to make another attempt. I'll act quick so it doesn't have time to take another chunk of my flesh. One ... two ... I pounce and grip the cat, swinging it over to me. It thrashes wildly like a fish being heaved into a boat. I hold it as tight as I can but, AARGH! I almost lose my balance and fall off, only stopping myself by whacking my head on the trunk.

Eventually, the cat calms down. I've got it. Relief washes over me. I'm kind of proud of myself, too. A year ago, there's no way I'd be able to climb a tree like this. I wouldn't have even been able to walk up to it. I take a moment to give myself a little pat on the back. Not literally. If I take so much as a finger off this cat it might chew my face off.

'Right,' I say. 'Let's try and get down without killing ourselves, OK?'

I begin to gently lower myself onto the branch below when—

'JORDAN MICHAEL TURNER, WHAT ARE YOU DOING UP THAT TREE?'

Oh. No. Nooooo.

'GET DOWN FROM THERE,' Mum shrieks. 'Wait, don't. I'm calling the fire brigade.'

'Please don't!' I yell. 'I can get down myself.'

'Like fiddlesticks you can!' she says. 'Don't go anywhere. I'll get the ladder.'

How could she only have been at the shop for five minutes? Does she do everything at three million miles an hour?

Mum disappears around the side of the house and then comes back with a ladder and sets it up against the tree. 'OK, climb down, but for the love of all that is holy, BE CAREFUL.'

I'm about halfway down when she notices the cat I have wedged under one arm. Thankfully, it seems to be paralyzed with fear.

'Put that thing down this instant!' she cries, but I ignore her. I know cats are supposed to have nine lives, but I'm still not dropping it from this height.

When I get to the bottom, she grabs the cat and puts it down and it instantly sprints away. Before I can move, she's grabbed my wounded hand.

'Did that animal do that? Oh my God, why would you help a vicious thing like that?'

I would tell her about the promise I made the best part of a year ago, but she wouldn't understand. She doesn't understand anything.

'I've a right mind to have a word with next door about their dog,' Mum says later as we pull off down the drive, headed for the hospital. I'm strapped into my child seat. Yeah, that's right. A *child seat*. I'm thirteen years old and my mum makes me sit in a child seat, like some kind of overgrown toddler. And yes, that includes when she drops me off at school. Fitting in at a new place where you don't know anyone is bad enough without turning up looking like you still go number two in your Huggies.

The hospital is an hour's drive away. It used to be just down the road, but since we relocated to Pondstead, it's a real mission. This is the first time I've been back since the move. It's actually my first check since I went into remission. I have to come back every six months to make sure . . . to make sure everything's OK.

The entire way there, Mum constantly sucks on mints, unwrapping them one-handed with trembling fingers. She always does that when she's nervous.

Mum doesn't have the radio on, so I put my earphones in and listen to my favourite playlist. I know every word to every song. I must have dropped off at some point, because the next thing I know, we're there. Mum pops the last mint in her mouth and turns around.

'Ready?'

'What if I say no?'

Mum tuts. 'Come on. While you're in there, I'll get them to check you haven't caught cat rabies.'

I don't have to go down to the children's ward, which is a relief. Instead, I'm in an outpatient clinic on the fifth floor. We're sitting in a boring waiting room, where classical music drips out of the speakers like treacle. There's a pile of magazines on a table and a few babies' toys in the corner. Nothing for me to do, in other words.

I think about what lessons I'm missing today. Science, Maths, History, PE. Pretty good going. If I'm going to miss lessons, might as well make it the worst ones. I don't even have to do PE, either. I just stand there and occasionally help Miss Stack put cones out. It beats having to play rugby but does nothing to get rid of my label as the weird new kid.

'Jordan Turner?' A nurse I don't know sticks her head around a door.

Mum and I get up and follow her. This next bit is routine. First, she measures and weighs me. Then she puts this tight, inflatable band around my upper arm and sticks a needle in the fat vein on the underside of my elbow. Some people get freaked out by needles, but I'm used to it. At this point, I'm like some kind of voodoo doll.

Once the nurse has a little vial of blood, she puts a plaster on me and sends us back out to the waiting room to do more waiting. Now, there's another thing I'm used to. Waiting. Waiting for doctors, waiting for visitors. Wait, wait, wait.

Mum fidgets with a magazine. I can tell she wishes she'd brought more mints. Meanwhile, I get the urge to wander the corridors, find my way back down to the children's ward. Would Kate remember me? They get so many kids in there they must all blend into one. But I know it wouldn't be the same if I went back. It couldn't be. But . . . I don't know.

Being back here spins me out.

I close my eyes and try to stop imagining the lab people examining my blood and seeing the numbers shoot back up. I picture more chemo, more throwing up, my hair thinning again. It's a familiar dark alley that my mind takes itself down again and again, and I'm powerless to do anything to stop it.

When the doctor calls us in, I try to steady myself and ignore the heavy, aching bowling ball of dread in my stomach. Mum squeezes my hand to try and reassure me, but I keep looking ahead.

I know the doctor. He was my consultant when I was on the ward. His name is Dr Kanelos. He's a nice, jolly man with lots of grey hair and a neat beard. As we sit down in his office, he fixes us with a thin smile. Not a full smile, but one where his lips are drawn in a little. What could that mean? It could be that it's good news. Then again, it could be a smile of sympathy.

I grip the edge of my seat. It's hard plastic, all bobbly. It might be the most uncomfortable chair I've ever sat in.

'So, Jordan,' says Dr Kanelos. 'Nice to see you again.'

I nod, too nervous to be able to respond properly.

'How are you feeling, in general?' he asks, but before I can do anything, Mum jumps in.

'He was running a fever of forty point eight before we came,' she says, her words coming as fast and frantic as an escaped Jack Russell. 'Then again, that's probably because he was up a tree, playing with a wild animal.'

'I wasn't playing with it,' I manage to croak. 'And it was a cat. A cat's not a wild animal.'

'Well, it spends its life outside. Sounds pretty wild to me.'

'It belongs to the old couple over the road,' I say.

'Well, look at what it did to his hand?' She grabs my wrist and holds it up for the doctor to see. 'Would a tame animal do something like this? What do you think, Doctor?'

Dr Kanelos shifts in his seat. 'Well, it's not really my area of expertise,' he says, then moves the conversation on. 'Besides the temperature, how are you feeling, Jordan?'

'He has headaches a lot,' says Mum. 'He's irritable all the time, too.'

Dr Kanelos nods. 'That's normal. Going back into the real world after such a long stay in hospital can be a tough transition. Headaches and mood swings can be symptoms of stress.'

Mum chuckles under her breath. I know what she's really thinking. Whenever me or my older sister Abi so much as think about the word 'stress', Mum appears as if from nowhere and yells, 'STRESS? YOU DON'T KNOW THE MEANING OF THE WORD!' It's like her superpower.

'I'd recommend plenty of exercise,' says Dr Kanelos. 'Get out on your bike, play sport, things like that.'

'But I've been keeping him off PE at school because I didn't think he'd be up to it,' says Mum.

'There's no need,' says Dr Kanelos, still smiling. 'Exercise is the best way to build your strength back up. Of course, Jordan, if it gets too much, stop. But there's no harm in easing yourself in.'

'Hang on,' I say. 'So, like, I'm OK?'

Dr Kanelos laughs, his eyes twinkling. 'Yes, I probably should have mentioned that sooner. Your bloods are absolutely fine. You're doing great.'

My body fills up with relief like warm water flooding into a bath. But then, something else overtakes it. A sour feeling in my stomach, radiating up to the back of my throat. Before I can stop myself,

I'm crying. Oh my God, this is so embarrassing.

Dr Kanelos slides a box of tissues over to me and I take one. Mum puts her arm around me, and I can tell without looking at her that she's crying, too.

'I know, it can be overwhelming,' says Dr Kanelos.

I suppose to look at me, you'd think I was crying tears of happiness. But I'm not. They're tears of guilt.

CHAPTER 2

'A toast,' says Dad, holding up his glass of squash. 'To Jordan's continued good health.'

Everyone joins in: Mum with her water, me with my smoothie, and Abi with a cup of herbal tea that makes her pull a funny face every time she takes a sip.

'Yeah, congratulations, little bro,' says Abi. 'Hey, now he's OK, can we go back to our old house?'

Mum tuts, clearly sick of talking about 'our old place' all the time. 'You know that house is sold, Abi.'

'Besides, don't you prefer it here?' says Dad. 'It's so peaceful.'

'No, I don't,' Abi huffs. 'There's no life in the suburbs. No culture. How am I going to become an influencer in the armpit of nowhere?'

'An influenza?' says Dad, trying not to laugh. 'What's that?'

'It's someone with loads of Instagram followers that gets sent free stuff,' I reply.

Dad shakes his head and sighs. 'I don't understand this world anymore.'

'That's not what it is, Jordan, and you know it,' Abi snaps. 'It's a way of leaving your mark on the zeitgeist.'

'I left a mark on the zeitgeist once,' Dad says. 'After that, they wouldn't let me return it to Ikea.'

I laugh. Every now and then, Dad's jokes are alright. Abi's not so impressed, though. She throws her fork down.

'I can't wait to go to uni next year,' she says. 'Get out of this one-horse town.'

I chuckle. 'I'm not keen on Pondstead either, but it's not a one-horse town.'

'Why?'

I point at the window, where on the other side of the fence, literally staring into our kitchen, are two horses.

Dad roars with laughter and high-fives me. 'Nice one, son.'

'Ugh, you are so literal-minded,' Abi says, getting up and taking her plate to the sink.

'Where are you going, young lady?' says Mum.

'Leave her, Claire,' says Dad. 'She's got to go and influence Instant-Gran.'

Abi mutters something under her breath and stomps up to her bedroom. She does that a lot, especially since we moved away from the city. And I get it. She's had to leave all her friends behind and she reckons that nobody at her new college is anywhere near as cool. That's not such a huge problem for me. All my time in hospital pretty much lost me my best friend, Ross. Though it gained me a new one. For a while.

I think Abi blames me sometimes. She's never said as much, but I can tell. After all, if it wasn't for me and my stupid defective blood, we'd still be living in our old house in the city, and she'd be free to experience as much culture as she likes. Not only that, but Dad wouldn't have to commute all that way to work every day and he wouldn't be so tired all the time. He's been an accountant for a magazine for years, way before I was born.

'Anyway.' Dad drums his hands on the tabletop. 'I've got a surprise for you, my boy. Follow me.' He gets up and makes his way outside.

Mum stares after him, her eyes huge. 'Surprise? What are you talking about, Graham?'

I follow Dad out to the shed, Mum trailing behind me.

'Your mum told me what the doctor said about you getting more exercise,' says Dad.

'Gentle exercise,' says Mum, folding her arms. 'I'm not having him play rugby. It's barbaric.'

Dad chuckles. 'Be that as it may, I picked you up a little something on the way home.'

He opens the shed door, and inside is a shiny, green mountain bike.

'What is that?' Mum pushes past us to stare at it.

'It's a bike, Claire,' says Dad. 'Think of it as two unicycles welded together.'

'Wow, thanks Dad,' I say, but Mum barely lets me speak.

'Where did you get it?'

'Ted in the village sold it to me. Hardly used.'

Mum leans over and squeezes one of the brakes. 'I can see why. The thing's a death trap.'

Dad ignores her and wheels the bike out of the shed. 'Why don't you hop on, take her for a test drive?'

Despite Mum's anxious jabbering, I get on. It's ages since I've been on a bike, but after a wobbly start, I manage to ride it out of the garden on to the cul-de-sac Now, this is fun. I feel the wind blowing through my hair as I pick up speed, hopping off the kerb. The hills are sprawled out in the horizon, reaching for the clear blue sky. I think about freedom. I think about the future. I think about Rio.

NEW KID

Being sick has some upsides, I suppose. Dad just bought me this new iPad to keep me entertained. It's got loads of movies downloaded onto it. Shame I can't watch them. I seem to have lost all my concentration in this place. The beeping, the nurses chatting, the weird, slightly off-looking Mickey Mouse painting on the wall grinning at me like it's going to come to life and eat my face. It's all a bit off-putting.

For something to do, I've decided to write down everything that happens while I'm here. It might be the only thing that keeps me from going mad with boredom.

It's getting late now, and Mum, Dad, and Abi have gone home. I start my treatment tomorrow. The doctor came around and explained things to us, but it just sounded like noise to me, like it wasn't real. I guess I'll find out when it happens.

There are three other kids in my little section of the children's ward. The two opposite me are younger, probably reception age. My mum, being nosy, found out they're only in for a little while: one of them for something to do with her ears, the other to have his tonsils out. I wish I was here for something like that. In and out. As it is, I'll probably be here for a month, maybe more.

There's another long-termer in the bed next to me. When we came in, she was staring at her tablet, frowning with her tongue poking out of the corner of her mouth. She had a pair of big headphones on, so I doubt she even knew we were there. She was also completely bald, so likely in for the same thing as me.

When Mum, Dad, and Abi had gone down to the café for lunch, she came over, dragged the big chair around so it was facing me and sat down. I already felt weird about being in bed in the middle of the day, and she wasn't helping.

'New kid,' she said, her voice flat and her expression giving nothing away.

'Um, hi.'

She narrowed her eyes at the board above my head. 'Jordan. Not sure how I feel about that.'

'What do you mean?' I shifted uncomfortably,

wondering if I should be sitting up for this? Reclining felt odd. I decided to compromise and go for this weird half-sitting position that hurt my back.

She cocked her head to one side like she was examining me. 'I don't think it suits you. Jordan makes you sound like the hardest kid on the estate. And that's not you.'

Is it that obvious? I thought. It was difficult to tell how old she was, but I'd say she is probably about my age, if not slightly older. She has big, light brown eyes which are a little bloodshot.

'You look more like,' she stopped and tapped her chin thoughtfully. 'A Dan. Or maybe an Ollie. Yes, Ollie. I like that one.'

I shrugged. 'Sorry. I didn't have much choice in it.'

She drew her legs up and sat yoga-style in the chair. 'You can always change it.'

I laughed a little. It seemed like she was joking, even though her face was deadly serious. 'So, what's your name?'

'Rio,' she replied.

I didn't have a comment to make about whether it suited her or not because I don't think I've ever met a Rio before.

'Oh,' I said. 'Like Rio de Janeiro?'

She wrinkled her nose. 'No, my Mum just really likes Duran Duran.'

'Who?'

She gawped at me. 'You've never heard of Duran Duran?'

I shook my head.

'You're so lucky,' she whispered. 'They are *rubbish*.'

'So are they a band or something?'

Rio made a fart sound and rolled her eyes. 'Kind of. Way too pop for me, though. I prefer more alternative stuff. My older sister recommends me all the best bands. Who do you listen to?'

I started to panic. All of a sudden, I forgot every musician that ever existed. My brain grasped around in the dark, desperately trying to remember anyone that has ever sung a song in their life.

'Oh, you know,' I said. 'All kinds of stuff.'

Rio narrowed her eyes at me again. 'I should introduce you to my sister, Simone. She'll sort you out.'

'Is that what you were doing earlier?' I ask, nodding at her bed. 'Listening to music?'

'Making a playlist for my mum,' she said. 'It's my thing. I make playlists for people.'

'Hey, maybe you could make one for me?' I said. 'Improve my taste in music.'

She folded her arms. 'Nah, I only make playlists for people I love, and no offence, pal, but we've only just met.'

Ah. I didn't know what to say. I felt like Rio had built her own world around that bed and it would take me a while to get used to all its customs.

'I heard them saying what you're in for,' she said. 'Snap. Except mine's in my bones.'

She said it so calmly, you'd think she was talking about a cold.

'Oh,' I said. 'So, have you had the chemo?'

'Nah mate,' Rio replied slapping her scalp. 'I just fancied rocking the Nick Fury look.'

I felt my face burning up. It was a stupid question, really.

'Yeah, I got Simone to buzz it all off when it started falling out,' she said. 'I don't want a comb-over like my grandad. You going to do the same if the time comes?'

I touched my hair. I'm hoping it won't come to that. 'Maybe,' I said.

A nurse marched over to us. 'You should be resting, both of you. Come on, Rio, back to bed.'

Rio smiled sweetly at her. 'I'm just welcoming Ollie to the ward.'

'His name's Jordan,' the nurse replied.

'For now,' said Rio, ominously.

The nurse rolled her eyes. 'Back in that bed in five minutes, or you and I are going to fall out.'

'What's the matter with her?' I whispered to Rio once the nurse was out of earshot again.

'Kate's having a bad day,' she replied. 'I heard her at the nurse's station earlier. Split up with her boyfriend.'

I raised my eyebrows.

'Yeah, I don't miss a thing round here,' she went on. 'Got to do something to pass the time.'

Before I could reply, the little girl in the bed opposite mine had woken up and started crying. Her dad had just gone, probably to go to the toilet or get a drink, and she must have been scared. Straight away, Rio jumped out of the chair, went over and sat next to her. I couldn't properly hear what she was saying, but she picked up a couple of superhero action figures from the table and started putting on a little play, which quickly made the little girl stop crying. She kept it up until her dad came back, then came back over to me and perched on the side of my bed.

'That was really nice of you,' I said.

Rio bobbed her head. 'It's all part of my new philosophy.'

'Philosophy?' I asked.

Rio leaned in closer to me, like she was letting me in on a deadly secret.

'There was a rabbi here yesterday,' she said. 'You know, like a Jewish priest kind of deal.'

I nodded, not sure where she was going with this story.

'We got to chatting and he told me about "mitzvahs",' she said. 'Do you know what a mitzvah is?'

'Isn't it a party where you get loads of money and people carry you around on a chair?' I said.

Rio shook her head. 'That's a *Bar* Mitzvah. A mitzvah is like a religious commandment, but it's also just doing something kind for someone.'

'OK,' I said, still confused.

'Well, I've been thinking about it,' she said. 'I was thinking that if everyone did mitzvahs for people whenever they got the chance, they'd pass them on and do more mitzvahs, and in the end, the whole world would be doing nice things for each other.'

To begin with, it sounded mad, but the more I thought about it, the more sense it made. I mean, when someone does a nice thing for you, it makes you feel better. Why wouldn't you want to pass that on to someone else?

'Yeah, sounds good.'

'I know, right?' said Rio, a smile lighting up her face. 'So why don't we test my theory out by doing something nice for Moody Kate over there?'

Now I really saw where she was going. 'OK, like what?'

Rio jumped off the chair, then went back to her bed, reappearing a few seconds later with a couple of pieces of paper and a pencil case.

'We make her a card,' she said.

'What kind of card?' I replied. 'Like, "Sorry you split up with your boyfriend"?'

Rio shook her head. 'Too on the nose. How about, "Thanks for being great"?'

We quickly got to work making the card. I did the lettering, while Rio drew pictures of the two of us, holding flowers. She'd just finished drawing the inside illustration when Kate reappeared.

'What are you still doing here, Rio? I thought I told you to go back to bed.'

'Sorry, Kate,' said Rio, handing her the card. 'We were just making you something.'

Kate sceptically took the card, but when she looked at it, she started to smile, and her eyes went all twinkly.

'Thank you,' she whispered.

Rio glanced at me, a little smile on the corners of her lips.

'Look,' said Kate. 'Maybe you can stay up for a little longer. But only five minutes, OK?'

'That's very kind of you, Kate,' said Rio.

When she left, Rio looked at me with her hands out, like a magician revealing the grand finale of a magic trick. Then we watched as Kate stopped by the other beds in our bay, taking time to laugh and joke with the families.

'Wow,' I whispered.

'I know,' Rio whispered back. 'The magic of the mitzvah.'

I'm pretty sure she is the cleverest person I've ever met.

CHAPTER
3

I coast down the road into central Pondstead,
the early morning breeze running through my
hair. Well, it would be if I wasn't wearing this
ridiculous helmet.

Now, please don't think I'm dissing helmets.
They're important. And I don't fancy bashing
my brains in on a lamppost any time soon. It's
just, this helmet Mum made me wear isn't even a
bike helmet. It's more like a motorcycle helmet,
covering my entire head and face. Racing green
with two white stripes. It's the only way I'm
allowed to bike.

Oh, and here's another new thing she's insisted
on: I have to take a flask of soup with me to school.
Apparently, it's full of vitamins and nutrition and
it'll give me enough energy to do PE and blah,
blah, blah— and she knows because she made it

herself. Hmm. I think it's staying in my bag, thank you very much.

Mum stood in the doorway watching me leave, and when I got to the end of the street, she was still there.

Even though I look stupid, it's still preferable to being dropped off at the gates in the child seat, so I take what I can. It's been ages since I've properly been on a bike, and even though my legs are already aching, it feels great.

Pondstead is a biggish town with a retail park and a cinema and stuff like that. Most of the kids from school live here, but nearer the centre than me. Abi moans that there's no 'culture' or whatever, but I think it's alright.

I pedal past houses with neatly trimmed front lawns and freshly washed cars gleaming proudly. The flower display at the roundabout won some kind of award, apparently.

I was so distracted by the scenery that I didn't notice all the other kids walking to school around me.

'Nice wheels, Helmet!' shouts Maxwell Foster, earning an explosion of laughs from all his hangers-on.

I can feel my face going hot, but I try and show

I'm a good sport by giving a little wave, but taking my hand off the handlebar makes me lose control and I nearly go into the back of an enormous Year Eleven kid.

I stare straight ahead and steer the bike into the school drive. I chain it up in the shelter, next to Raven and Aurora (real names Amelia and Heather) who always hang around there listening to heavy metal and looking miserable.

'Nice headgear,' Raven mumbles, as I yank the helmet off and attempt to smooth down my duck's bum hair.

A bit rich coming from someone with an 'I Eat Babies' beanie hat, but I decide to maintain a dignified silence and head into school, where I quickly stow the stupid thing in my locker.

I look around and sigh. Everyone is huddled together, chatting and laughing, and I'm on my own. Why is it so hard to make friends? It never used to be like this. Back in primary school, it was like, 'DO YOU LIKE PEPPA PIG? GOOD. WE'RE FRIENDS NOW.' That's how I met my old best mate, Ross. These days, it's like there's an invisible wall between me and the rest of the world. I talk different to everyone here. I don't know the town that well. You'd think I'd moved to an entirely different country rather than an hour up the road.

I've been here nearly six months, but I still haven't told anyone about my illness. I don't know why. I guess I've just never found the right way to bring it up. 'Oh, you like football? That's interesting. I had cancer.' It's awkward, is what I'm trying to say.

And it's not only that. It's like . . . It's like I've forgotten how to let people in. There have been times that people have asked me to do stuff after school, and I've made excuses to not go. And I still don't know why.

'Hey.'

I turn around to see Maxwell leaning up against his locker, arms folded, his eyelids halfway down his eyes like the shutters on a shop.

I nod and mumble something at the floor. Maxwell Foster is the most popular kid in our year, to the point where he's almost like a celebrity. I have no idea how he does it. He's just got this way about him that makes people gravitate towards him. He's like a magnet but with really cool hair.

'What you doing at lunchtime?' he says.

I shrug and say, 'Not sure yet,' even though I know full well I'm going to eat lunch as quickly as possible, then sit in the library until it's over. Standard procedure.

'Want to come to the chippy with us?' he asks.

I gulp because I know who 'us' are. Us is Maxwell and Imran and Will and Daria. The cool kids. They're like the Avengers. Oh my God, do they want me to join the Avengers? Maxwell is clearly Cap, and I reckon Imran is Iron Man, so maybe I could be the Hulk? I've had enough toxic stuff inside me, after all.

He's still looking at me and I haven't answered yet. *Don't go, Jordan*, that vaguely Mum-sounding voice in my stupid brain warns. *It could be a trap.*

I blink hard to try and wipe it out of my head like a squished moth from a windscreen. I've already ridden a bike this morning, why can't I go for lunch with some people?

'Yeah, I'll come to the Hulk,' I say.

Maxwell splutters with laughter. 'Hulk?'

Oh Goddddd.

'Yeah,' I nod really quickly. 'It's what we call the chippy where I'm from.'

Phew. That was pretty smoothly done, I thought.

'Nice one,' Maxwell chuckles. 'Meet us at the gate at one, yeah?'

I'm still nodding. I'm not sure I can stop. 'Sounds great.'

CHAPTER 4

I'm telling you, they're just messing with you, says my stupid brain. *They're going to lure you out of school and pelt you with eggs.*

'Shut it, idiot,' I grunt.

'What did you just say?' a massive Year Ten lad huffs at me.

ARGH! STOP TALKING TO YOUR BRAIN OUT LOUD, YOU MORON.

'Nothing,' I say, using the crowds to my advantage and shimmying away from him before he can pound my city-boy face into gravy granules.

It's lunchtime. I haven't been able to concentrate during any of my lessons. I've gone backwards and forwards on whether to go or not, and I've finally decided I'm going to do it. What's the worst that could happen?

They could strip you naked and cover you in gone-off

mushy peas.

Shut up.

They could roll you up in a carpet, drive you to a suspension bridge and throw you into the river.

Shut. Up.

I get to the gates and the whole gang is there. They're all staring at me.

Your fly is probably open. Best check.

'Watch where you're putting your hands, Helmet,' says Will, making everyone laugh.

I look at the floor and stuff my hands in my pockets. Then I put them by my sides. Then I fold them. What do I normally do with my hands, anyway?

Maxwell puts his arm around my shoulder and guides me out of the gates. 'Glad you could make it.'

'Yeah,' said Imran. 'Shame you're not wearing that sick helmet, though.'

See? They're going to whack you on the skull with a crowbar.

Daria laughs. They were with Maxwell this morning when I went past on my bike. Before that, I'm pretty sure they didn't know I existed. Daria jabs me on the arm. 'We noticed you sit alone a lot, so we thought we'd invite you along.'

Will hoofs a pebble, which ricochets off a lamppost and hits my leg. 'Cos we're some kind of charity, apparently.'

'Leave it, Will,' said Maxwell, in a tone of voice that made it seem like it wasn't the first time they'd talked about it.

'So you're from the city, right?' said Imran. 'That's cool. You must be minted.'

'Not really,' I say. 'We didn't live in a super fancy area or anything.'

'Yeah, but still, the *city*,' says Imran. 'Must suck to end up here.'

'No,' I blurt. 'No, it's, you know, it's alright.'

Will makes a fart noise. 'Sounds like you think you're better than us.'

I don't know what his problem is. I don't think we've ever spoken before today. But he clearly doesn't like me very much.

'Ignore him,' says Maxwell, swinging a playful punch at Will. 'He's just in a bad mood cos Miss Stack dropped him from the football team.'

'Am not,' Will shoots back. 'I don't even care about the stupid team. Anyway, shut up, I'm too busy thinking about chips.' He nods at George's Fish Bar on the corner.

'You like chips, Helmet?' he goes on. 'Or do you only eat caviar?'

I ignore him and fumble in my pocket for my change. I can scrape together just enough for a burger and a can of Coke. Mum would be horrified if she knew I was eating stuff like this. I hope she won't be able to smell it on me.

I follow the gang across the road to the park, where they all sit under a tree. Will, who has spent about a tenner and has so much stuff it could feed all of us, points at a tent with his battered sausage.

'I see our mate's still here.'

Maxwell laughs. 'I'm surprised, after what you did to him yesterday.'

Will sniggers and rubs his hands together. 'If he's going to camp in the park, he should expect a bit of disruption.'

'Can't believe you threw rocks at his tent,' says Daria. 'You're such a villain, Will.'

Will chucks a chip in the air and catches it in his mouth. 'The best bit was when he tried to chase me. I could crawl quicker than him.'

I don't know who they're talking about. I've only been in this park a couple of times before and the tent wasn't there, then.

Imran shakes his head. 'That was cold.'

'You know what?' Will sits upright. 'You're right, Imran. That was cold. I must be making a terrible impression on our royal guest.' He bows down to me. 'I should go and apologize.'

Maxwell shares a look with Imran and Daria. 'Whatever, man.'

Will jumps to his feet, chips still in his hands. 'Watch me.'

'Here we go,' Maxwell mumbles.

Will walks across the park to the tent and shoots us a half-smile. 'Knock knock!' he yells.

'Oh man,' says Imran, hiding his face.

The zip on the tent opens and a man sticks his head out. He looks neater than you'd expect for someone living in a park—he's clean shaven, short cropped hair. He's younger than I thought, too. Maybe thirty-something.

He says something that sounds like, 'What do you want?' but I'm not sure.

'I've come to say sorry.' There's no mistaking Will's words. He's talking loudly, like he's acting in a play. 'I was out of order.'

The man mumbles something.

'Would you like some chips?' says Will.

The man mumbles something else.

'You'll have to speak up. I can't hear you!'

'Yes please,' says the man.

Will holds the chips out to the man. The man reaches out his hand, but then Will snatches them back, because of course he does.

Maxwell starts laughing, but then catches himself and shakes his head. The man doesn't do anything as Will runs back to us. He just goes back into his tent and does the zip back up. But before he does, I catch the expression on his face. It's tired and sad.

'Mate . . .' says Imran, letting one word do all the talking.

'What?' says Will, shovelling a handful of chips into his mouth. 'I'm just having a bit of fun with him. He looks like he needs cheering up.'

'We'd better start heading back,' says Daria. 'I don't want to be blamed for terrorizing a homeless man.'

Everyone gets up and starts the walk back, but I stay behind. How can we just leave him? Shouldn't someone say something? Maxwell seems like the leader of the group. I feel like he should put things right. But he's not. He must notice I'm not there at some point, because he stops and looks at me.

'You coming, Jord?'

'No,' I say, my voice coming out all pathetic and wobbly. 'I've, um, got to go to the shop. For . . . something.'

Maxwell looks confused. 'Oh. Do you want us to wait for you?'

'No,' I say. 'I'll see you back at school.'

I hear Will snigger and whisper something to Imran.

'Alright,' says Maxwell. 'See you around.'

They keep looking back at me as they walk away, and I try not to give away that I have no idea why I've stayed behind or what I'm going to do.

Nicely done. My first shot at making friends since You Know Who and I've blown it.

I try to concentrate. I remember the promise I made. I have to stick to it. I walk over to the tent and take a deep breath.

'Um, hello.'

I hear shuffling inside. 'Go away,' he says.

'I just wanted to say sorry for Will,' I say, even though I'm not sure why I'm apologizing for someone who's not even a friend. 'He's an idiot.'

The man grunts. 'You have ten seconds to leave. I

am trained in armed combat.'

Oh. I'm about to turn and run, but then I remember something. I open my bag and pull out that flask of Mum's soup. There's no way I'm going to eat it, and this bloke seems like he's hungry.

'Ten . . . nine . . . eight.'

I put the flask down in front of his zip. I think about saying something, to let him know it's there, but I decide not to. If he judges me by Will's standards he'll probably think I've spat it in or something. Best to let him find it.

'Seven . . . six . . . five.'

As I walk away, I feel the tension of the afternoon evaporate. Rio was right, back then. It feels good to do a mitzvah.

PINKY SWEAR

I've only been in hospital for two days but we've already done three mitzvahs.

1. Read stories to little kids
2. Collected all the dirty plates
3. Tidied the rec room

Pretty easy stuff, but it passes the time. Anyway, earlier on, after Mum had gone home and I'd texted my best mate Ross for the tenth time with no reply, Rio came over to my bed.

'I've had an idea, Ollie,' she said. 'It's a big one.'

'What is it?'

'I don't know if you're ready for it,' she said. 'I mean, it'd be a big commitment.'

'Go on,' I said, intrigued now.

She looked around like she was anxious an eavesdropper might steal her idea, then leaned in close. 'It's a year of mitzvahs.'

I raised my eyebrows at her, which she took as a cue to explain further.

'You and me spend an entire year doing every mitzvah we can. Whenever someone needs help, we step up. It is FORBIDDEN to walk away when there is an opportunity to do good. It doesn't matter if it's your worst enemy, or a grumpy old man, or, I don't know, a cat stuck up a tree. And when we do it, people will want to do mitzvahs for others, and so on. Then, we meet up exactly a year from today and see if we've changed the world.'

I thought about it for a second. To begin with, my instinct was to be selfish. I mean, I've got enough going on in my own life without trying to help others. But there's something so persuasive about Rio that I can't help but think it really is the best idea I've ever heard.

'OK,' I said. 'I'm in.'

Rio held out her little finger, hooked slightly. 'Pinky swear.'

I grip her finger with mine. 'Pinky swear.'

CHAPTER
5

I open my eyes and look around. How did I end up back here? The white ceiling, the disinfectant smell, the menacing Mickey Mouse on the wall.

I turn to my left, but Rio's bed is empty. Of course it is. I find the nurses' button and press it twice. I need to know how I ended up back in hospital. My memory is a blur. Did I collapse at school?

I press the button again and again, desperate for someone to come. But no one does. I sit up to see if there's anyone opposite. That's weird, the beds aren't there anymore. Why would they take beds out of a ward?

I drag myself up. Everything hurts. I feel like I've been run over. Oh my God, maybe I was. Maybe Mum was right about the bike. I climb out of bed and look out of the window. It's black out there.

No light at all, not even from street lamps. I catch a glimpse of my reflection and a wave of nausea hits me. My hair is gone. I touch my fingertips to my scalp. This doesn't make sense. None of it does. I need to speak to a nurse. Is Kate still here?

I stagger across the room to the corridor. It's empty. The only sound is the buzzing of the fluorescent light tube above my head. When I get to the nurses' station, I see Kate. She's got her back to me, but I can tell it's her. Thank God. She'll be able to tell me what's happening.

'Kate!' I croak.

She doesn't move. I must not be loud enough. I move closer and call her name again. She still doesn't move. When I'm near enough, I reach out and touch her shoulder. It feels cold. She spins around but she doesn't have a face. There's just a shadow.

'Kate?' I yell.

The shadow ripples and twists, getting bigger and bigger, coming right for me. I try to run, but my legs don't work, and I have an IV line in my arm and the darkness is coming, the darkness is coming.

BEEP BEEP BEEP BEEP BEEP.

My alarm is buzzing. I'm sitting up, drenched in sweat. I'm sick of these nightmares. They're becoming more and more common now. Nearly every night. I take a few deep breaths and try to convince myself that they won't last forever. They can't. Can they?

After splashing my face with cold water in the bathroom sink, I head downstairs and start making breakfast. I'm hoping to get away without having to listen to Abi's nonsense. It's the last thing I need after another nightmare. No such luck.

'Just look sad,' she says, sticking her phone in my face while I try to eat my toast.

'Leave me alone,' I say. 'I don't want to be on your stupid Instagram.'

'My feed is far from stupid, dorkus,' she says. 'You know just the other day, I received a DM from a total stranger telling me I'd changed her life.'

'What happened? Did you inspire her to never go on Instagram again?' I say.

Abi flicks my ear. Ow. How does she make that sting so much?

'That's more like it,' she says, snapping a photo of me. 'Hurt and afraid.'

I get up and take my plate to the sink. 'Why do you want me on there anyway?'

'Because I'm trying to get across to my followers

how this heinously cruel move has affected my entire family.'

I groan. I wish she'd give it a rest. She's been relentless since we moved here. Pondstead's not as bad as she makes out. I mean, it's not as if it's the middle of nowhere. There's a McDonalds.

'Cool it with the negativity, Jordan,' she goes on. 'I get enough of that at college. Did I tell you about my strike?'

'You went bowling?'

'Not that kind of strike, you wand. Industrial action. Taking a stand.'

I don't say anything. She's going to tell me about it whether I like it or not.

'They announced that they were cancelling the Expressive Dance class,' she says. 'So I organized a strike. We were all going to walk out and refuse to participate until it was reinstated.'

'Why are you bothered? You don't do Expressive Dance.'

'That's. Not. The. Point,' Abi snaps, clapping with each word. 'The point is, I should have the choice. Anyway, my classmates clearly didn't feel as strongly because no one else showed up.'

I splutter with laughter. 'So you went on strike

by yourself?'

'Suburban people have no fight,' she says. 'It's like living amongst zombies.'

I'm about to head out when Mum intercepts me at the door. Dad leaves for work super early, which means I only have to avoid one parent in the mornings. Mission failed.

'And where do you think you're going?' Mum says, a flask of soup in her hand.

'Oh, right,' I say, reluctantly accepting it.

'This one is Mulligatawny. Very tasty if I do say so myself.'

What's Mulligatawny? Some kind of cat? Has she murdered that one I rescued from up the tree?

'Make sure you bring this one back, Mister,' says Mum, ruffling my hair. 'I can't be having you leave all my flasks at school.'

If she knew I'd given the last one to a bloke living in a tent in the park, she would flip her lid.

I cycle off, stupid helmet on, with Mum watching from the door. She never watches Abi leave. The other day Abi said to her, 'I could emigrate to Argentina and you wouldn't care.'

Imagine if Abi did emigrate to Argentina. At

least I'd be able to eat breakfast in peace. It wouldn't last long though. She's so annoying, they'd end up kicking her out.

'Hey, Jord,' Maxwell turns around in Maths while Miss Farley is outside. 'Coming for lunch today?'

I don't know what to say. I mean, I can't say I enjoyed it yesterday. Will makes me feel constantly on edge, like pushing a wheelbarrow full of dynamite through a sparkler factory.

'Don't worry about Will,' he says, as if he can read my mind. 'He can get a bit weird sometimes, but he's alright, mostly.'

I nod. 'OK. Where are you going?'

'Same again, probably,' he says. 'Wherever we go, it beats hanging around in this dump.'

Later, I'm back in the park and I wince when I see the tent still there. This time, everyone's been to the minimart for food. I'm about to sit down, but Will grabs me by the shoulders and moves me so I'm facing everyone else, then he sits me down.

'What are you doing now, Will?' says Maxwell.

'You lot want him to join our group,' Will says, sitting opposite me. 'But how do you know he can be trusted? He could be a spy.'

'What are you on about?' says Imran, chucking a Twiglet at him. It misses and hits Daria.

'Just saying,' says Will. 'I think we should grill him. Make sure he's legit.'

'You need to shut up,' says Maxwell.

Will ignores him and narrows his eyes at me like he's a lawyer and I'm in the dock for murder. 'Why did you move here?'

'My Dad's job,' I say, even though Dad has actually moved further away from his job. There's no way I'm giving them the real reason.

'Don't buy it,' says Will.

'What do you mean?'

'I watch this detective show and it tells you how to look out for deceptive body language,' says Will. 'When you answered my question, you touched your face.'

'Did I?' I say, and have to stop my hand from making its way upwards again.

'Yep,' says Will. 'So come on. Why are you really here? Did you do something so bad at your last school that you had to move?'

'Leave it now, Will,' says Maxwell.

Will holds up a hand to silence him. 'Please, Maxwell. How do we know this new mate of ours isn't a school arsonist or something . . . ?' He goes to say something else, but he's distracted by something behind me. 'Is that what I think it is?'

'It's a tent,' says Daria.

Will stands up and shields the sun from his eyes. 'No, not the tent, that thing next to it.'

I turn around, relieved that the focus is off me, and I think I see what he's talking about. It's about half a metre long with silver edges that glint in the sunlight.

'It can't be,' Will whispers in a voice filled with awe, like he's just uncovered an ancient treasure chest.

'What are you talking about?' says Imran.

Will ignores him and walks over to the tent. He's focused on whatever that thing is. I don't know what it is, but I don't like how excited he is.

He holds it aloft, a massive grin on his face. 'I knew it!' he mouths.

Oh my God, it's a leg. OK, not a real leg, but a prosthetic one. It must belong to the man in the tent. That explains why Will said he couldn't chase him the other day. Wait, what's he doing?

Will's running away. It looks like he's heading for the pond. No. He can't. I don't even think about it. I'm up and chasing him across the park. He looks over his shoulder and shoots me a smug look, but doesn't change course. I can't let this happen.

He reaches the water's edge and holds the leg above his head. Before he can throw, I call out to him. He turns around, a little grin playing on the corners of his mouth.

'Everything alright, Helmet?'

I shake my head and try to get my breath back. 'Don't do it.'

'Do what?' says Will. 'I was just doing some exercise with it, that's all.' He tries to look confused, but his mouth is still twisted into that smirk. 'What did you think I was going to do with it?'

'I thought you were going to throw it in the pond.'

Will clasps the leg close to him and his mouth drops open in shock. 'What a terrible thing to think, Helmet. The thought never even crossed my mind. But now you've given me the idea.' He wags his finger at me. 'I'm going to have to do it.'

'No!' I make a grab for the leg, but he wrenches it away and flings it into the pond, where it lands with a splash, before floating on the surface.

'Why did you do that?' I yell. 'What's wrong with

you?'

Will steps close to me. So close, he's all I can see. 'I don't like you, Helmet. You don't belong here. So if Maxwell asks you to come out with us again, you make an excuse. That clear?'

I step away without answering his question. That won't be a problem. Being alone is my default setting. Besides, why would I want to hang out with them anyway?

Will says some other stuff to me, but I'm not listening. I'm too busy trying to work out how to get that leg back. I can't wade out into that pond; it's too deep. Maybe I should just leave it. I'm sure that guy can get another leg from somewhere.

Yeah right, imagine what Rio would say if I did that. I can't go back on the pinky swear. It is FORBIDDEN to walk away when there is an opportunity to do good. There's a big branch lying next to some bushes. That might be long enough to drag the leg out. I stand as close to the water as I can, my shoes sinking into the boggy mud, but it's just a little too far out. I look back at where the rest of the gang is sitting, but I can see them getting up to leave. Surely one of them will come over to help?

Doesn't look like it.

There's only one thing for it: I'm going to have to lie flat on my stomach. It's the only way the stick will reach. I curse Will under my breath and get down in the mud. It's cold on my chest and I shiver as I sweep the stick across the surface of the water and catch the leg. Slowly, I manage to drag it closer until I can pull it out altogether. My shirt is filthy and my sleeve is thick with green pond slime. I hope this bloke appreciates what I've done for him.

I'm approaching the tent and about to put the leg down and run when the zip flies open and the man lunges out, hopping up onto his one foot.

'What you doing with my leg?' he barks.

I step back. His eyes are wild and intense. He's bigger than I thought, too.

'I'm sorry,' I say. 'This other kid threw it in the pond and I got it out.'

His eyes dart down at my mud-covered chest. I notice he has lines on his face, like he's just woken up. 'Right,' he says, holding his hand out. I pass him the leg and he puts it on the ground and fastens it on. It's weirdly fascinating. I've never seen someone put a fake leg on before.

'My own fault,' he says. 'I shouldn't have left it outside.'

He squints at me and scratches his jaw. 'You're the kid I was talking to yesterday, aren't you?'

I nod.

'You leave me that soup?'

'Um, yes?' I don't know why I say it like it's a question, but what's done is done.

'Thanks,' he says. 'It was really nice.'

Huh. How about that? Mum's soup is alright after all.

'Talking of soup,' I say, reaching into my bag and pulling out the other flask. 'I've got another batch, if you want?'

The man nods, then goes back into the tent and fetches me the old flask. 'Cheers,' he says, taking today's soup. 'Name's Harry.'

'Jordan.'

'You make nice soup, Jordan,' he says.

'It's actually my mum,' I say.

Harry takes the lid off the flask and sniffs. 'Well, your mum does, then. Wish my mum was still around to make me soup.'

I don't know what to say to that. Mum drives me crazy, but if anything happened to her, I'd miss her like mad.

'There's other people like me in town, you know?'

he says. For a split second, I think he means other one-legged people, but then I realize he means homeless. 'They'd love good stuff like this.'

And that's when I get an idea. An idea that might be the greatest mitzvah ever.

So chemo sucks. I don't know why I'm surprised by
that fact, but man. *Man*. I feel like I've been hit by
seven lorries. This is the first time I've felt well enough
to write since I started.

This is how it works. They hook up a drip into
my arm which has this poison in it. The poison
is supposed to kill the cancer cells in my blood.
Sometimes, I close my eyes and imagine the poison
attacking the cancer, hacking at it, destroying it.

While the drip is in, it's not that bad. Just a bit
sore, that's all. It's when it comes out that's the killer.
It was about two hours later when I started throwing
up. I wanted to go to the bathroom and do it, but
the nurses wouldn't let me, so I just had to sit in bed
and barf into what looks like a cardboard hat. Mum
rubbed my back, when she wasn't panicking to the
nurses that I was dying. And Rio dragged a chair over

to the side of my bed. I really didn't want her to. It was embarrassing. I wanted to stop throwing up, but I couldn't. Even when everything was gone, my stomach was still convulsing.

'It's alright, mate,' she said, softly. 'Better out than in, that's what my granny says.'

She reached over and held Mum's hand.

'Don't worry, Ollie's mum,' said Rio. 'Vomming's normal. He'll stop soon.'

'His name is Jordan,' said Mum, confused.

'If you say so.'

Rio was right. I did stop. For a while. Then I had the urge to go again, but this time all I brought up was this horrible yellow stuff which burned my throat. I know this is disgusting to read about, but I guess cancer is disgusting.

Kate—who had been chuckling to herself for most of the day after Rio said she was a 'strong, independent woman who don't need no man'—made me drink some water, even though I knew it would be coming straight back up. And guess what? It did. Every time. It was like trying to hold a float under in a swimming pool. By the end of the night, I managed to keep down half a slice of toast and a couple of sips of water. And that was when the aching started. My back, my knees, my elbows, even my eyes. I'd go to pick my iPad up, but the simple movement sent electric forks of pain through every inch of my body so I could do nothing but lie there and stare at the ceiling.

'You're in the Puke Pit,' said Rio.

'The what?' I croaked.

'The Puke Pit.' She repeated it like it should have been obvious. 'When the chemo makes you constantly feel like you're about to puke.'

'Oh,' I said. 'Yeah, that sounds about right.'

She sat at the end of my bed. 'Take a long breath in through your nose.'

I did as she told me.

'Now let it out through your mouth.'

I released the breath slowly.

'Keep doing that, and try to only think about your breathing. Imagine the air you're breathing in to be blue and the air you're breathing out to be red. Picture yourself slowly becoming more blue than red. Honestly, it sounds kooky but it helps.'

I closed my eyes and tried to only think about breathing. It's weird, really. You're always breathing, but you never have to think about it. Your body just does it. It's odd to actually concentrate on it. Nevertheless, I tried. I pictured myself as being hollow, like a chocolate teddy bear, but filled with red sand. With every breath, a little of the red sand seeped out and a tiny amount of blue filtered in.

I was amazed that it actually helped. I felt lighter and the pain was much less intense. When I was finally blue, I opened my eyes. Rio was still there.

'Thank you,' I whispered. 'It really worked.'

Rio nodded. 'Course it did. Consider it a mitzvah from me to you.'

CHAPTER
6

Mum looks at me like I've sprouted a head from my armpit.

'You want me to make soup for all your friends?'

I nod. 'They love it. They say you're a genius. A soup genius.'

Mum folds her arms and narrows her eyes at me. I can tell she doesn't buy it. 'Hang on a minute. Since when are teenagers into soup?'

'Didn't you know?' I say. 'Soup is like . . . the big thing, now. If you go on Instagram, it's hashtag oxtail, hashtag minestrone. All the influencers are going crazy for it.'

'Hmm,' says Mum, doubtfully. 'Maybe I'll ask Abi about that.'

'Thing is,' I say quickly. 'Only the top influencers are into it. Abi is too small-time. And I'm not just saying this, but my friends say your soup is the best they've ever tasted.'

Mum blushes a little. Oh, my God, is this working? 'OK,' she says. 'Maybe I can rustle up some small portions for Monday.'

Dad walks in and grabs an apple from the bowl. 'When are you going to rustle me up a little smooch?' he says, winking at Mum and taking a big bite. Of the apple, I mean, not Mum. Dad's always in a better mood at the weekend, but I wish that didn't involve him being so disgusting.

'Oh, you.' Mum giggles. 'Anyway, did you hear? Jordan's making friends at his new school.'

If only they knew.

'Course he is,' says Dad. 'He's a charming young man. Hey, Jord. Any of these friends of yours chicks? Do young people still say chicks?'

'No, we do not,' says Abi, appearing in the kitchen doorway as if she was waiting for something to complain about. 'Because it is degrading to women.'

Dad shoots me a 'yikes' look and changes the subject. 'Anyway, you fancy coming to the cinema this afternoon? I hear there's still a few tickets left for that new Marvel film. That is, unless you're going with all these new mates of yours?'

'No, that'd be good,' I say. I'd been wanting to see

that for ages.

Dad toasts me with his apple and turns to Mum and Abi. 'How about you two? Fancy coming and watching the Avengers beat up Stavros, or whatever his name is?'

'No thanks,' says Mum. 'Not my kind of thing. Besides, I'll be too busy making soup for half the school.'

'How about you, Abigail?' he says.

Abi rolls her eyes. 'I hardly think that would be a valuable use of my time. I *will* take a lift into town, though. I'm planning on doing some shooting.'

'I don't think you're old enough to possess a firearm,' says Dad.

Abi groans. 'Just let me know when you're going, OK?'

We park up outside the cinema. At least once I've watched this film, I'll be able to join in some conversations at school. It's all everyone's talked about for weeks.

As we're about to get out of the car, Dad turns around to Abi. Yeah, I'm allowed in the front when Dad drives. It's nice to be out of my baby chair.

'So, what are you going to be up to while we're watching the film?'

'I've had an idea for a new series on my YouTube

channel,' she says. 'It's about having to leave the city and live in the suburbs. I'm going to show the world what it's like existing in a place that doesn't have falafel.'

Dad nods sympathetically. 'Well, if enough people hear about your plight, they might pull together and record a charity single for you. Maybe put on a big concert at Wembley Stadium? Instead of 'feed the world' it will be 'feed Abi falafel.'

Abi climbs out of the car. 'I'll make my own way home,' she says.

We go inside and Dad gets us a massive popcorn to share and a couple of drinks each. And he doesn't even moan about how much it costs.

'This is nice,' he says. 'You and me spending some time together. Father and son bonding.'

Five minutes later, he's fast asleep and snoring through the trailers. He's so tired these days.

On the way home, we drive past the park. I crane my neck to try and see Harry, but I can only just make out the roof of the tent. When I do, I'm filled with excitement. The film has made me feel like I can save the world singlehandedly, like a superhero.

No, wait.

A *souperhero*.

CHAPTER 7

I'm fully aware that this is a nightmare. Usually these things seem dead real, but this time I know I'm lying in my bed in my haunted bedroom and my brain has taken me back to the hospital ward.

Not that this knowledge makes it easier to escape. I'm stuck here. And I can't change the dream. I can't transport myself to Disney World or a tropical beach or a sunny meadow. I'm standing in the corridor with that smell clinging to me like mould. My hair is gone again, but this time there are scaly scabs on my scalp, sore to the touch.

'Ollie?' Rio's voice echoes down the corridor, from the rec room where the TV is. I've never seen Rio in one of these dreams before, even though I've desperately wanted to. I take off in her direction as fast as my bony legs will take me. I open the door to the rec room, but inside, it's the MRI room. The big scanner clicks and whirs, almost drowning out Rio's cries.

'Help me! I'm stuck in here!'

I look around and see a big red button on the wall. That must shut the whole thing off. I mash it with my palm and the machine winds down.

'Thank you,' she says. 'Now help me get out. I've been alone here for so long.'

I go to the head of the MRI. I've only had to go in one of those once, and I hope I never have to again. It's like being trapped in a tubular coffin.

I look into the opening. I can't wait to see Rio again. But . . . that's not Rio. Because instead of a face, there's that yawning black void again, but this time it zooms out, consuming me. I thrash my limbs and scream, but it crushes every part of me and I can't breathe and—

'Jordan!' I open my eyes and Mum is standing over me, holding my shoulders.

'Were you having a nightmare?' she asks.

'No,' I say, then, realizing I'd have no way to explain why I was probably screaming and thrashing, decide to tell the truth. 'Yeah, I was.'

Mum puts the back of her hand across my forehead. 'You're not running a fever, at least. Maybe

I should call the doctor, just to be on the safe side.'

'No,' I say. 'Just a bad dream, that's all. I'll be fine.'

She surveys me doubtfully for a minute and then pops a mint into her mouth. 'Anyway,' she says. 'I've nipped down to the supermarket and bought some more flasks for your school friends. They were on offer! They're a bit much for you to carry, especially when you're under the weather, so I'll have to give you a lift.'

Great.

So here I am, trying to clamber out of my baby seat before anyone can see me. What a life.

'Hello, Jordan!' Will swaggers over to the car. Oh man, here we go.

'Hello there,' Mum calls from the window. 'You must be Jordan's friend. Are you the one that likes my soup?'

'Your what?' Will splutters with laughter.

'No, not him,' I say, getting out of the car and heaving my heavy bag onto my shoulder. 'He's allergic.'

'Why are you lying to your mum?' says Will, and I want nothing more than to grow to the size of a skyscraper and hoof him into the sun.

'I'm going to be late,' I say. 'See you later, Mum.'

'Wait!' Mum calls urgently, like she's just seen the school go up in flames. I turn around.

'What about my kiss?'

Thanks, Mum. Thanks a lot.

I don't look at Will and walk fast to the gates, trying to lose him in the crowd, but he catches up with me easily.

'So here he is,' he says. 'The hero.'

'Leave me alone,' I mutter.

'No way,' says Will. 'I can't believe I'm standing this close to Pondstead's answer to Superman.'

I pick up the pace, but he's right next to me, getting close to my face and grinning.

'BA-BOW!' Will makes an explosion noise. 'He's here to rescue tramp's legs from the briny deep, but he's not too big and strong to give his old mum a goodbye smooch.'

I stop dead and stare at him. 'Go away.'

'Make me.'

He looks back at me, his face completely blank. 'Well go on, then.'

I try and step around him but he blocks my way. I try the other way but he does the same thing. I go shoulder first, trying to barge him, but he's big and solid and I get nowhere.

'Come on, you're supposed to be a hero.'

I don't know what I'm supposed to do.

Oh. Oh, no.

Will laughs like he can't believe what he's seeing. 'Dude, are you crying?'

I quickly touch my face and sure enough, it's wet. What? Why am I crying?

Will shakes his head. 'If I'd known you were going to be such a baby about it, I wouldn't . . .' He trails off and looks around like he's nervous about being caught. 'Alright, see you around, Helmet,' he says, before stalking away.

I sneak off into the toilet and splash my face with cold water. That has never happened before. Yeah, I've cried but not without warning. Normally, I'll get that lump in my throat and my vision will go all swimmy. This time it just came on like a tap.

At lunch, I grab a panini from the dinner hall and eat as I walk, little spots of grease dropping onto my shirt. I'm walking fast because I want to get to Harry before Will and the gang do. I have no doubt Will's told them about me randomly bursting into tears and now they all think I'm insane.

I find Harry sitting outside his tent. It's a warm afternoon and he looks like he's enjoying the sun.

'Alright?' he says, with a smile.

'Hi Harry,' I say. 'I brought some soup for you and your friends.'

He raises his eyebrows at me. 'Oh right. That's proper nice of you.'

He seems kind of uneasy, like he's not used to people being kind to him. I have to put him at ease, like Rio would.

'Do you want to show me where they are then, Harry?' I say.

Harry frowns for a couple of seconds, but eventually nods. 'Alright.'

He turns around to zip up his tent, and as he does, I catch a glimpse of the inside. I'm shocked at how neat it is. His sleeping bag is tightly rolled and his things are filed away in three bags sitting in a perfect line. He must notice me looking because he nods and says, 'I'm ex-army. Old habits die hard, you know what I mean?'

Makes sense. I suppose when you live such a restricted life, it's hard to give it up.

'Is that how you lost your leg?' I ask. As soon

as it comes out of my mouth, I cringe. I could have worded it better.

'Yeah,' Harry replies, matter-of-factly. 'Iraq. IED.'

I've heard about IEDs. They're these bombs left on the ground like traps. I imagine stepping on one and my skin goes all prickly.

'Anyway.' Harry's voice goes all quick and loud, like it did the day I brought his leg back from the pond. 'That was in the past, and we don't live in the past. Stay here. I'll go and fetch the guys.'

Without another word, he heads off in the direction of the park gates.

I look around, nervous that Will and the others will show up. How will I explain what I'm doing? I pull a cap out of my bag (Mum makes me keep it in case the sun is too strong) and pull it down low.

Within a couple of minutes, I see some figures making their way towards me. At least it's not Will. It's Harry, along with a young girl, probably a little older than Abi, along with a woman about Mum's age, pushing an old man in a rickety wheelchair.

'This is Jordan,' says Harry when they arrive, 'the lad I was telling you about.'

The old guy, who has a shaggy, white beard and a

white sailor's hat on his head barks, 'SOUP BOY?'

'Yeah,' says Harry. 'Jordan, this is the Captain.'

The old man salutes a greeting.

Harry points at the older woman. 'This is Elaine.'

'Alright?' she says.

'And this,' he says, pointing at the younger girl, 'is Daniela.'

Daniela nods at me and smiles thinly. Her cheeks are sunken, like she hasn't eaten properly in weeks. Man. I take the soup out of my bag.

'How lovely,' says Elaine, reaching into a plastic bag hanging off the handle of the Captain's chair. 'I've got some bread to go with it, too.' She hands out rolls to everyone.

'Where did you get these?' Harry asks.

'The skip round the back of Safebuys,' she replies. 'I was going to get more, but the security guard came out and chased me off.'

Harry rolls his eyes, as if it was something that happened all the time.

'Why did they chase you away?' I ask, as I begin to hand out the flasks.

Elaine shrugs. 'It's their property.'

'What, old food they're throwing out?' I say. 'That's mad!'

'Pigs!' the Captain yells.

'Too right,' says Harry. 'They'd rather send stuff to the landfill than feed people in need.'

They seem to accept it as a fact of life, but to me it's the most unfair thing I've ever heard.

It goes quiet while they tuck into their soup, dipping the bread into their cups.

'This is lovely, Jordan,' says Elaine.

'Best soup ever,' the Captain agrees.

Harry dunks his roll in it, then chucks it into his mouth. 'What did I tell you? The stuff is unbelievable.'

'Do you make this?' Daniela asks.

'No,' I reply. 'It's my mum.'

Daniela gets this sad look on her face then and takes another sip of her soup.

'Well, tell her from me, she's a saint,' says Elaine.

There's no way I'm ever going to tell her. If she knew I was standing in a park with four homeless people, she would die of a heart attack, come back to life, die of a heart attack again, come back to life for a second time, then explode in a ball of flames.

Still, as I watch everyone enjoying the soup, I realize that I feel more relaxed with them than I do with Will and the rest of the gang. Then the Captain accidentally drops his bread on the floor and screams the loudest, most disgusting swear word I've ever heard.

When I get home, I text Ross and ask him what he's up to. I know we're not as close as we used to be, what with me now living absolutely miles away, but there's no reason we can't stay in touch.

Four hours later, he still hasn't replied.

I know Mum and Dad care about me, I get it.
That's why they're here all the time. But they are
EXHAUSTING. Mum is always fussing about whether
I'm drinking enough water or whether I'm getting the
right amount of my meds, and blah, blah, blah. And
Dad is doing his Weird Dad act. Case in point:

'So how's my favourite dude today?'

He never says 'dude'.

'You look great, really on the up.'

This was right after I'd finished puking.

I feel like telling him it's alright to say nothing
sometimes.

Still, at least today they had someone else to speak
to. Dad was in the middle of setting up a board game
on my table when Rio's parents walked in. I hadn't
properly met them before. When they'd visited other
times, I'd been too out of it to register them. I don't

think Mum and Dad had met them before, either.

'Oi, oi!' yelled Rio's dad. 'How's my princess?'

He was wearing a football shirt that looked like it was from way before I was born, and there was an enormous green dragon tattoo snaking its way up his hairy arm.

'Still trapped in the tower,' Rio replied as her dad kissed her bald head. 'Where's Mum?'

'She's coming,' her dad replied with a big sniff. 'Just fetching your surprise from the car.'

Mum and Dad stopped talking. I could tell they were listening to what was happening. They couldn't help it, really; the bloke was like a foghorn.

'What surprise?' Rio said.

Her dad let out a sly chuckle. 'If I told you, it wouldn't be a surprise now, would it?'

Before Rio could say anything else, a woman I guessed was her mum: blonde hair piled into a beehive and a T-shirt with 'Wine O'clock' on it, crept around the corner like a cartoon burglar.

'Afternoon, sweetheart,' she said, her voice wobbling with mischief.

'Why are you acting so weird?' said Rio, glancing at me through the corner of her eye.

'Because I've got your surpri-iiiise,' she replied, all

sing-songy.

Rio sat up. 'Well come on, what is—Oh.'

I followed Rio's gaze to our bay entry. Standing there, smiling hugely, was a girl who was probably about eighteen or nineteen. She had loads of multicoloured wristbands up her arm and she was wearing a T-shirt with 'Velvet Underground' written on it. Oh, and she was completely bald, too.

'Simone, you're back!' Rio cried. 'What's happened to your hair?'

'Me and my mates at uni shaved our heads for Cancer Research,' she replied, as she walked over.

This must be the sister she told me about that knows loads about music. Wow. Shaving your head when you don't need to is dedication.

'Rubbish,' said Rio. 'You're just copying my wicked style. Hey,' she leaned forward and pointed at me. 'This is Jordan-slash-Ollie.'

Simone looked at me with a smile. 'Hi Jordan-slash-Ollie! I've heard so much about you.'

I shot Rio a look. What did that mean? What had she been saying?

'Oh, how rude, we haven't introduced ourselves, yet!' said Rio's mum, turning to my parents. 'I'm Sandra and this is Kev.'

Mum and Dad quietly but politely told them their names, but it quickly became clear that wasn't going to be enough for Rio's parents, who came clattering over, arms open for big hugs.

'I'm surprised you don't recognize my voice!' said Rio's dad, rubbing his hands together.

Mum and Dad shook their heads. I could tell they didn't know what to make of him. He cleared his throat and started singing. 'Braddock's Bathrooms, here for you, we'll fit your shower and your loo!'

'Oh,' said Dad. 'Is that you?'

Rio's dad threw his head back and laughed. 'Did you hear him? Is that me?' He pulled a business card out of his pocket and pressed it into Dad's hand. 'If you ever find yourself in need of a wet room, give me a call. Very reasonable.' He winked at Mum.

'Oh, Kev, why are you always thinking about work?' said Rio's mum, giving his arm a playful smack. 'Tell you what, how about we all go out for lunch later? Our treat?'

'That's very kind,' said Mum. 'But we've—'

'Nonsense!' roared Rio's dad. 'It will be our pleasure.'

'Besides, we've been in and out of hospital with our Rio for years, so we thought you could do with some pointers,' said Rio's mum.

Mum and Dad looked at each other. I could tell that they were trying to think of an excuse but couldn't conjure one up between them.

'That'd be lovely,' said Dad, with a forced smile.

Once the parents had gone, Rio and Simone sat around my bed.

'We're here for an opinion, Ollie,' said Rio.

I put down the book I was supposed to be reading for English. It's a Shakespeare play about a load of fairies and a bloke with a donkey's head. At least I think so. It might be the chemo making me hallucinate.

'OK?'

'It's Simone's demo,' said Rio. 'I really like it, but I think she needs the perspective of someone who's not really into music.'

'But I am into music!' I said.

Rio nudged Simone with the back of her hand. 'Mr "I like all kinds of stuff" over here. It's fine not to be into music, Ollie. Most people aren't that into music. That's why we need you. You represent the masses.' She passed me her tablet, with earphones plugged in.

'Honestly, Jordan, ignore her,' said Simone. 'I'm just keen for as many people to hear it as possible.'

I liked Simone already. She has a kind face and

looks like she's always smiling. I pressed play. Her band's name is The Inside Out and the song is called 'Stargirl'. It starts off slow, with just a soft guitar, and then her voice comes in. It's really nice. She's a great singer. I realized they were both staring at me and I wasn't sure what to do with my face. Do I smile? Do I look serious? I decided to look at my bedsheet and try to ignore them. The chorus goes:

You are my stargirl,
Forever by my side.
Shining bright through the blackest
    of nights.

When it had finished, Rio sat back in her chair, arms folded. 'So what do you think?'

Now, here's the thing: even if it was three minutes of a goat farting, I'd still say I enjoyed it. But I didn't have to lie. 'Really good,' I said. 'Like, brilliant.'

Simone blushed a little and looked at the floor. 'Thank you, Jordan.'

'See,' said Rio. 'The normies love it. You'll be headlining Glastonbury in no time.'

'Normies?' I said. 'Am I a normie? What's a normie?'

'There's no shame in it, Ollie,' said Rio, carefully

climbing out of her chair. 'It just means you're a regular person. I'm a bit jealous, really. Right, I need to use the little girls' room.' And with that, she began the trip to the end of the corridor where the girls' toilets are.

'Sorry about that,' said Simone, running a hand over her head, like she was still getting used to being bald. 'My little sis can be a bit demanding.'

'That's OK,' I said. 'I really did like the song.'

Simone smiled even wider. 'Thanks. It's a special one.'

'Is it about her?' I asked.

I'm normally quite shy around people I don't know well, but there was something about Simone that put me at ease.

'Is it that obvious?' she asked.

'Not obvious,' I said. 'I could just kind of . . . I don't know, sense her in the song. Does she know?'

Simone shook her head. 'I haven't told her. I've got a feeling she might have an idea, though.'

I bet she does. She's clever.

'Rio likes you, you know,' said Simone, lowering her voice.

This time, I blush.

'I know she has a funny way of showing it,' she went on. 'But she really does. She has a hard time making friends, probably because she's spent so much time in hospital, but trust me, she's glad you're around.'

It's really embarrassing, but when she said that, my throat went all tight and my eyes stung. I just nodded a bit because I knew if I tried to talk, it'd come out all strangulated and weird.

'She tells me she's got you involved in the mitzvah thing,' said Simone. 'Me too.' She pointed to her bristly scalp. 'I've never met someone quite so persuasive.'

Just then, Rio appeared from around the corner. 'You been talking about me?'

CHAPTER 8

'There you go,' says Mum, lining up the flasks. 'It's a good job I enjoy making soup, otherwise this would become a chore.'

'Thanks, Mum,' I say. 'My friends will really appreciate this.'

Mum sits down at the table with her mug of coffee. 'I can't believe young people are so into my soup. I wonder what it is? It might be the combination of spices I use. I've been told they're very popular right now. Very "in".'

'If you say so,' Abi grunted from behind her book.

'And what's that supposed to mean?' says Mum, raising an eyebrow.

'It's supposed to mean I don't buy it,' says Abi. 'I think Jordan's doing something else with the soup.'

I shoot her a look. 'What am I doing with it?

Throwing it at old ladies?'

Abi shrugs. 'I'm just saying, I don't know any young people *that* into soup. And I know what young people are into.'

I groan. 'For the last time, Abi, you are not an influencer. The last time you tried to make a video, you ended up getting chased by an angry mob.'

'I hardly think five people is a mob, Jordan,' says Abi. 'And besides, that was only because they couldn't handle the truth.'

The truth being that she asked them what it's like living in a 'cultural wasteland' and they didn't like it.

'I'm going to keep an eye on you, dearest brother,' says Abi, wagging her finger at me. 'Because I've got a feeling you're keeping something from me.'

On the way into school, flasks crammed into my bag, I spot Will in the distance, so I slow down, then take the long way round and go in through the other entrance. If I can just avoid him every day for the next four years, I'll be sorted. I'm about to congratulate myself in making it to class without seeing him, when I nearly run straight into Maxwell.

'Hey, Jordan, I've been looking for you,' he says. 'How come you didn't come out with us yesterday?

You didn't let Will put you off, did you?'

I know they couldn't have heard what he said to me, but surely they must know stealing a homeless man's prosthetic leg isn't normal behaviour?

'Kind of,' I say, feeling self-consciousness hit me like a falling piano as I realize Maxwell probably knows about the weird crying moment. 'But anyway, I can't leave school at lunch for a while because I've got detention.'

'Detention?' Maxwell chuckles. 'What for?'

I notice my hand creeping up towards my face, but I quickly slap it back down to my side. 'Just didn't do my Maths homework, that's all.'

'Harsh,' says Maxwell. 'Well, maybe see you when you're a free man, then?'

'Yeah,' I say. 'Maybe.'

At lunch, I again make sure to rush out of school before Maxwell and Co can get out. This time, I meet Harry down at the loading bay, along with the Captain, Elaine and Daniela.

'Afternoon!' I say. 'The Soup of the Day today is carrot and coriander.'

'Bleugh,' says the Captain. 'Don't like it.'

Harry laughs. 'Looks like beggars can be choosers. Well if you don't want it, we can share it between us.'

The Captain thinks about it for a second, then grabs a flask. 'OK, I'll have some.'

'Thought so,' says Harry.

Elaine takes a sip and closes her eyes. 'Another triumph,' she says. 'I used to love making soup before . . .' She trails off, letting the word hang in the air.

It goes quiet for a while, with everyone enjoying their lunch. I unwrap my sandwich and start eating along with them. There's something nice about providing a hot meal for people who don't normally get one. Man, Rio would get the biggest kick out of this.

Hmm. You know in *Star Wars* when they sense a disturbance in the force? Well, that's how I'm feeling right now. Like I'm being watched. Oh no. Has Will tracked me down? I look up at the entrance to the loading bay, shielding my eyes from the sun, but the hazy figure doesn't look like Will. It looks older. And like a girl. It's coming closer. Oh. Oh, no.

'So these are your friends, are they?' says Abi.

CHAPTER
9

'You followed me here?' I whisper-shout at Abi as I spring to my feet. 'What's wrong with you?'

'I'm just a big sister looking out for her baby brother,' she says. 'So how long has this been going on?'

'Mind your own business.'

Abi raises an eyebrow at me. 'Hey, I'm totally fine with all this. I'm just not sure Mum will be so understanding.'

'Alright, fine,' I snap. 'Just a few days.'

'Who are you?' says the Captain, eyeing her suspiciously.

'It's OK, Captain,' I say. 'It's just my sister. She's going now.'

'Am not,' she says, stepping towards the group. 'Hi, I'm Abigail and I'm a filmmaker.'

'You are so not a filmmaker,' I say.

'I'm a filmmaker,' she says again, firmer this time. 'And I would love to document what is happening, here.'

'You gonna pay us?' says Harry.

Abi smiles. 'There's no budget at the moment, but if we can get some big investors on board, who knows?'

'Hold on a second,' I say, stepping between them and trying to regain a scrap of control. 'What are you talking about?'

Abi sighs, still smiling. 'I sometimes forget you're not a creative genius like me. The way I see it, this project, if you could call it that, is worthwhile for three obvious reasons. One: it highlights a societal issue.' She points at the gang. 'Two: it shows what good work you are doing and will encourage others to do the same. Three: philanthropy is going to be the next big thing in influencer circles, and I want to be ahead of the curve.'

I have no idea what that last one means, but I can't help but think she has a point about number Two. The whole point of the pinky swear was that mitzvahs should encourage other mitzvahs. But then again, mine and Rio's thing has never been about drawing attention to ourselves. I don't know what to think.

'What about Mum?' I say, grasping at something that might put the brakes on Abi for a while.

'There's no way she'll find out,' Abi shoots back. 'It's not as if she's much of an Internet person. She's not even on Facebook, like all the other olds.'

I try to argue, but Abi bypasses me and walks straight up to the gang. 'So, how about it? Do you guys want to be in a film?'

'My favourite film is *The Wizard of Oz*,' says the Captain.

Daniela shrugs. 'OK. Whatever.'

'So, what, it's a film about soup?' says Elaine.

Abi smiles. 'Only in the sense that *Citizen Kane* is a film about a sledge.' She stops for a second and I can almost hear her brain whirring. 'It's actually going to be about the sense of community around the soup. About finding hope in desperate circumstances.' She shakes her head, as if she's amazed at what she's come up with while I cringe myself inside out.

'So you're saying it's about more than just soup?' says Elaine.

'Exactly,' says Abi, clapping delightedly.

'Hang about.' Harry steps forward. 'Making a

film is all well and good, but how's it going to help us?'

This time, Abi is stumped. It's pretty obvious she was only thinking about how to get more fame as an influencer. As much as I hate to do it, I have to bail her out. It's kind of a part of the whole pinky swear deal.

'You could say something about Safebuys I suppose?' I suggest.

'Yes!' Elaine gives me a thumbs up.

'Safebuys?' says Abi. 'The supermarket?'

'They threaten to call the police on homeless people that take stuff they were throwing out anyway,' I say.

Abi's eyes go huge. 'What? But that's outrageous! And behind the times, too because all the Le Petit Boulangerie branches in the city have been giving away unsold food for ages. Man, this place really is stuck in the past.'

'Too right,' says Elaine.

'We've got to do something about that,' says Abi. 'We'll name and shame them!' She starts rubbing her hands together. 'This is going to be epic.'

Me, I can't decide whether this is going to be the best thing ever or the worst.

ROSS

Ross visited today. It was the first time I'd seen him in ages. He sat in the chair by my bed with his hands stuck in his coat pockets.

'Healthy kiiiiiid,' Rio droned at him like a zombie, arms outstretched.

Ross smiled nervously, his eyes lingering on her bald head.

'Want a drink or anything?' I asked him. I've got a supply of horrible fruit drinks in my cupboard I'm keen to get rid of.

'Nah.'

It went quiet after that. I could hear Kate at the nurses' station singing along with the radio.

'Your mate's a talker, Ollie,' said Rio.

Ross shot me a questioning look. 'Long story,' I say.

He shrugged and went quiet again. Rio got out of bed. 'As thrilling as this is, I'm off to see Kate, and find out if she's managed to snag a new boyf.'

I looked at my iPad propped up on my desk, playing to no one. I've downloaded this new series everyone's going crazy about, but the Puke Pit makes it hard to concentrate.

'What's it like?' asked Ross.

'I don't know. I can't really get into it,' I replied.

'No, not that.' Ross tapped the arm of the chair, gently. 'You know. Cancer.'

I couldn't help but laugh. 'It's the most fun you can ever have,' I said. 'Ten out of ten. Would recommend.'

Ross sighed a little and shifted in his seat. 'You're going to be alright, aren't you?'

I swallowed hard. 'Yeah,' I said. 'Yeah, I'm going to be fine.'

I don't know that for sure. I just try not to think about it. 'Look, all I ever talk about is cancer. You're supposed to be taking my mind off it. How's school? Mr Bletchley still a nightmare?'

'He left,' said Ross. 'Some people reckon he's quit teaching altogether.'

'Oh,' I said. 'Well that's good news, I guess.'

Ross shrugged.

'So who have you been hanging around with?' I asked.

'Reece and Ade mainly,' he replied. He must have

noticed my raised eyebrows because he followed it up with, 'They're alright, really.'

We'd never really got on with Reece and Ade before. We weren't into the same stuff. At times, they could be kind of mean. I'm surprised Ross would hang out with them.

'Oh, right,' I said. 'So what kind of stuff do you do with them?'

Ross shrugged. 'Football.'

I spluttered with laughter. 'But you hate football!'

'Do not,' he said, a little snappily.

'You do! We both do! We even made that comic together called *Football Sucks*'.

It's true. I still have it on my desk upstairs.

'I'm into it now,' said Ross, folding his arms. 'I support Arsenal.'

'Right,' I said, remembering how Reece and Ade were ALWAYS banging on about Arsenal. 'Are they good, then?'

'They're the best,' he huffed.

We descended into silence again. This was going to be a long afternoon.

Thinking about it, I don't remember ever seeing his hands out of his pockets the entire time he was here. Did he think he could catch cancer or something?

CHAPTER
10

DOWN AND OUT IN PONDSTEAD: A NEW VIDEO SERIES BY ABI xx

ABI: Hi guys. As you know, I left the city some time ago and have been trying to adjust to life in Pondstead. It's . . . different here. I mean, for one thing, the quality of sushi is abysmal. But there's one thing that is the same: the homelessness problem. Yes, even though the houses here are much cheaper, there are still lots of people with nowhere to live. Most Pondstead residents ignore these poor folks, but not my little brother.

The camera pans over to me. I groan and move away, but Abi puts her arm around me and pulls me into shot.

ABI: Yes, despite going through turmoil of his own.

ME: Alright, leave it now, Abi.

ABI: Despite all that happened to dear Jordan, he is determined to help others. Introducing: the Soup Movement!

ME: The Soup Movement? Since when is it called that?

ABI : Like our friend Elaine said, this is more than just soup. It is human kindness in a hearty, liquid form.

Abi moves closer to the gang and films me handing out the flasks. We all look super awkward.

ABI: In an ideal world, charity like this would not be needed, but in the imperfect society we find ourselves in, it's people like Jordan that are keeping things going.

ME: Alright, David Attenborough, steady on.

Abi films the gang enjoying the soup.

ABI: Each episode will feature an interview with one of the soup recipients. The first will be a chat with the lovely Elaine.

ELAINE: Not today, thanks.

ABI: Harry?

HARRY: Nope.

The camera abruptly cuts to the Captain sitting in front of a wall.

ABI: So your name is . . . the Captain?

CAPTAIN: Yes.

ABI: And what's your story?

CAPTAIN: Wha?

ABI: How did you end up in your present predicament?

CAPTAIN: . . . Wha?

Elaine moves into shot.

ELAINE: I think he might need some help.

ABI: So why is he called the Captain? Was he in the navy?

ELAINE: No, he used to live on a barge with his wife.

CAPTAIN: Maureen!

ELAINE: Yes, Maureen. But when Maureen passed away, the barge fell into disrepair and he had to be rehomed. But he didn't take well to living on land.

CAPTAIN: I need the water!

ELAINE: And, as you can see, he's not a well man.

CAPTAIN: Nope. No, no, nope.

ABI: Isn't there any way to get him somewhere to live?

ELAINE: They've tried, but he won't stay put, will you, my man?

CAPTAIN: Nah.

ELAINE: But I look after you, don't I? You, me and Daniela are like a little family. I know it sounds weird.

ME: No, I get it. When you're stuck in a situation with someone, you do become close.

Abi squeezes my hand.

ABI: Thank you for helping the Captain share his story, Elaine.

CAPTAIN: Thank you!

The shot switches back to Abi as she walks away from the gang.

ABI: That was episode one of what will be an ongoing series. Join me next time, as I go down and out in Pondstead.

THE BUSKER

I was emerging from a particularly bad trip to the Puke Pit when Rio appeared at the end of the bed like a ninja.

'How do you get over here so quietly?' I asked her.

'My creepers,' she said, holding up one leg to reveal a fluffy, rainbow-coloured sock. 'I glide as softly as a cloud in these bad boys.'

I sat up and stretched my arms out, trying to ignore the clump of hair left behind on my pillow. 'Very impressive.'

'Anyway, I'm off to the rec room. You coming?'

I agreed. I was finally well enough to leave my bed, so I thought I might as well make the most of it.

Down the corridor there's a play area with loads of old toys and picture books and Disney DVDs. The rec room next door is for older kids. There's a sofa and a TV and an Xbox. Only a 360, but it'll do. There's some

95

board games, too. Me and Dad usually have a game of Scrabble. I won the last game, but I'm pretty sure he let me win. I wish he wouldn't.

We entered the rec room and Rio closed the door and leaned against it like she was trying to stop me from leaving.

'What are you doing?'

'There's a reason I brought you here, Ollie,' she said, deadly serious.

'Why won't you just call me Jordan?'

'Now is not the time for questions, Ollie.' She grabbed my hand and dragged me over to the window. Her hand was warm, and I could feel all the little bones and tendons moving under her skin. I was surprised that I felt a little jolt of electricity whizzing up my arm as we walked.

Our ward is on the sixth floor, high above the street. You can't really hear the traffic, but sometimes I like to come here at night and watch the lights drift by. If I squint, it looks kind of magical. Sounds sad, I know.

Rio knocked the window. 'See him?'

There were dozens of people milling around on the pavement. 'You'll have to be more specific.'

'*Him*,' she said, tapping the window again. 'The

busker.'

I blinked hard a few times. The Puke Pit always gives me blurred vision. When my eyes finally cleared, I saw him. He was sitting on a little chair, playing the bongos.

'I've been watching him all day,' said Rio, 'and hardly anyone has given him anything.'

'Maybe he's really bad at the bongos,' I said.

Rio tutted and poked me in the side.

'Ow!'

'That's not the point. He's trying his best.' She leaned into me, her eyes narrowed. 'We need to take him something.'

'You're joking, right?' I said. 'We're not allowed out of here. It'd be easier breaking out of a high-security prison.'

Rio shook her head. 'Your lack of faith disturbs me. We swore to do as many mitzvahs as possible, didn't we?'

'Yeah, but—'

'And did we not agree that walking by when someone is in need is FORBIDDEN?'

'I know, but we've done loads of mitzvahs lately,' I replied. 'We got that little girl a present to cheer her up, we emailed that reality TV guy and got him to record a message for your mum's birthday. Can't we just chill for a while?'

'No,' Rio snaps. 'There is no time to chill. We have to think bigger. And besides. She folded her arms and jutted out her chin. 'The pinky swear is sacrosanct. It cannot be violated.'

'Alright,' I said, defeated yet again by the pinky swear. 'We'll take the stupid bongo man some money.'

CHAPTER
11

Another night, another nightmare. This time, I was chained to my hospital bed while the shadow people hovered around the room. A mirror descended from the ceiling, and when I saw my reflection, it was Will.

Even without the nightmares, I'm finding it difficult to sleep. You see, *Down and Out in Pondstead* has had ten thousand views. It's only been up for three days.

Abi tweeted it to a famous journalist, who ignored it, so she tweeted him again. And again. Eventually, he watched it just to shut her up, but was so impressed that he retweeted it, which got it retweeted by loads of other people, including other famous journalists. What really stuck a rocket under it, though, was the Captain. The Internet loved him, and people were angry that he could be left like that. There were articles and videos and all kinds of stuff.

People kept tagging Pondstead's MP, asking him how he could allow things like this to happen.

Another thing was that people were calling me a hero. Loads of people. I'm not a hero. This whole thing was just an accident, really. I only left Harry the soup because I felt bad about Will being an idiot. Now I'm being talked about like I'm some kind of saint.

I am sitting in my bedroom trying to take all this in, when Mum gives one of her patented door-knocks. I quickly change tabs on the laptop. She has no idea her baby boy is becoming such a celebrity.

The door opens and she sticks her head in. 'I've got a surprise for you!'

I don't like the sound of that. Before I can worry too much about what it is, Mum opens the door further and someone shuffles in, head down.

'Alright?' he mumbles.

I get up from my bed.

Ross.

'Ross's mum and I have been plotting this little surprise for weeks!' says Mum. 'He's going to stay over tonight. You should take him out, show him the sights.'

Huh. That won't take long.

I look at Ross. Why does he seem so different? It's not all that long since I last saw him, but he's bigger now. And it's weird, but he seems to stand differently. I don't know how to explain it. It's as if an alien has disguised themselves as Ross, but they haven't quite figured out the mannerisms.

'Well, this place might not be as lively as what you're used to, Ross, but it's not a compete ghost town,' says Mum. 'For example, did you know that today is Pondstead Day?'

Ross shakes his head. 'Didn't see it on my calendar.'

Mum chuckles. 'I'm not entirely sure what it's all in aid of, but there's going to be a fireworks display in the park tonight, so we're all going down. Anyway, don't let me keep you boys from having fun.' She stops, unable to help herself. '*Safe* fun.'

Wow. Safe fun. The best kind.

'So, how have you been?' I ask Ross.

He shrugs. 'Same old, you know.'

It's strange, seeing him here. Like, some kind of glitch in the matrix. Ross belongs in a package with our old neighbourhood; he's out of place here.

He goes over to the window and looks outside at the man next door painting his fence. 'What do you do for fun around here, anyway?'

'Oh, haven't you seen?' I say. 'I feed homeless people soup on the Internet.'

Ross nods, as if that makes perfect sense, then quickly shakes his head. 'Wait, what?'

An hour later, me, Ross, and Abi are back at the loading bay. Ross has his arms wrapped around himself and looks like he wants to run away.

'We need to capture the sense of community,' says Abi. 'But also, the sadness. Elaine, would you mind if I took a close-up of your trainers?'

'What's wrong with my trainers?' says Elaine, defensively.

They look like a strong wind would fragment them into a thousand pieces, but I don't want to say anything.

'I'll make you a deal,' says Elaine. 'You can show the whole of the YouTubes my old shoes if you do something about Safebuys.'

'Right!' says Abi, flicking my ear. 'Why didn't you remind me, Jordan?'

Ross huffs next to me.

'Everything alright?' I ask him.

He shrugs. 'I didn't realize I'd be coming here to hang around with tramps.'

I feel like my heart stops.

'Did he just say the T word?' says Harry.

'No!' I say, a bit too loud. 'He said . . .' I look around and see a slope leading up to the loading deck. 'Ramps! Ross is a skateboarder.'

Harry nods. 'Oh yeah. I used to do that when I was a kid. Bit hard now.' He lifts his trouser leg to reveal his prosthesis.

Ross stuffs his hands into his pockets and walks away until he's on the path by the main road.

'Your mate squeamish, or something?' says Harry.

'I don't know,' I say. 'I'll talk to him.'

I approach Ross, but he won't look at me. 'Everything OK?'

He sighs. 'I guess I just don't get it.'

'Get what?'

'This,' he replies, gesturing around. 'It's weird.'

'What, feeding homeless people?'

He looks like he's trying to think of something to say, but gives up, his hands flopping down by his sides.

I don't have chance to say anything else because Abi is marching over to us. 'Come on,' she says. 'We're going to Safebuys.'

I've been dreading this. When I first brought Safebuys up to Abi, I thought we would make one of those online petition things or something. I was stupid, really. We're talking about someone who organized a one-woman strike because her college cancelled Expressive Dance.

We follow Abi across the road, and around the back of Safebuys, squeezing through a gap in the fence. There are two huge skips against the wall, and they are full of food, most of it edible.

'Look at this,' says Abi, picking up a pack of croissants. 'The sell-by date was two days ago and they're being thrown out. This is an outrage.'

She's got a point. They're just going to be sent to the dump to rot, when they could feed people. It's an insult. The more I think about it, the more angry I become. I look at Ross to see if he agrees, but he's just shaking his head.

'Rooting through bins, now,' he says. 'Is this the fun stuff your mum was going on about?'

I remember a time when he would have been well up for an adventure like this. Like when we sneaked into that creepy abandoned house at Halloween. What's happened to him?

'Oi!'

We turn around and a burly man who looks like he was stitched into his shirt strides over to us. 'What do you think you're doing?'

Abi gets her phone out and starts filming. 'We're taking goods for the homeless.'

'Oh no you're not,' says the man. 'This is private property. Now sling your hooks, or I'll call the police.'

'This is INJUSTICE,' Abi yells. 'We shall not be moved.' And with that, she lies down on the floor. Oh God.

'You two,' she hisses. 'Get down here.'

Ross sticks his hands up and walks away. 'No thanks. I want to go home tomorrow, not be stuck in a prison cell.'

'Jordan,' says Abi, eyeballing me. 'We have to make a stand.'

Oh, man. I guess if I said no, I'd be going against the pinky swear. I hope you're happy, Rio.

I lie down on the disgusting floor and can hear the security bloke sounding like he's about to blow a gasket.

'Alright,' he fumes. 'If that's how it's going to be, I'll have to get the police to move you.'

Great.

'Hi guys, welcome to my livestream,' says Abi, holding her phone up in selfie mode. 'As you can see, we're lying on the floor outside Safebuys supermarket.' She points the camera at me and I give an awkward wave. 'And the reason for that is we have discovered that they throw their expired food away and threaten legal action on any homeless people that try to take it. Yeah, you heard that right. They'd rather throw food away than feed the hungry. So we're saying 'enough is enough'. We will not move until they have changed their policy.'

She starts singing 'We shall not be moved', but I don't join in. This is already embarrassing enough. I glance over and see Ross staring at us like we've lost our minds. Which, I don't know, maybe we have.

'We have a thousand people watching this and it's going up,' Abi yells between verses. She shows me her phone, and sure enough, the number is rocketing.

The security bloke stands over us, exasperated. 'Look, kids. I don't have any say over company policy. Just clear off and write a letter to head office, eh?'

'Never!' says Abi. 'You know as well as I do, that letter will be thrown away like so much expired brioche. The only way to change things is by direct action! Now either get out of our way or lie down with us.'

He sighs and runs a hand down his face, before turning and lolloping back into the store.

'What do you think he's doing?' I ask Abi.

'I think he's going to talk to his paymasters,' she replies, laying it on thick for all the livestream viewers. 'And they're going to bend to our will.'

'Come on, now,' says the policeman, standing over us. 'You've caused quite enough of a scene for one day.'

'That's where you're wrong, copper!' Abi yells back. 'We haven't even *started* making a scene. If you think this is a scene, you just wait, because it's going to be the biggest scene this two-bit town has ever witnessed!'

'Abi,' I whisper. 'Don't call it a two-bit town. I think he's got a club attached to his belt.'

'Don't make me ask again,' he says, with more than a hint of menace.

'Or what?' says Abi. 'We have a right to peaceful protest.'

I hear the policeman grumble under his breath. A muffled call comes through his radio, and he huffily replies, saying he might be a while.

'You might have the right to peaceful protest, my love,' he says. 'But you don't have the right to trespass on private property.'

'What's a bigger crime?' says Abi. 'Trespassing, or depriving the hungry of a meal?'

The policeman crouches, his face filling the screen, earning loads of angry emojis. 'Trespassing,' he says. 'Now come on, hop it before I call your parents.'

Well that's done it. I jump to my feet and run out of that place like the floor is lava. There's no way I want Mum finding out. She'd ground me until the sun burns out. I see Ross sitting on a bench over the road, so I go and sit next to him. Just as I do, he tuts and shoves his phone back in his pocket.

'You alright?' I ask, trying to calm myself down.

'No,' he says. 'My stupid mum is refusing to come and pick me up until tomorrow.'

'You want to go home now? Why?'

Ross looks at me like I'm crazy. 'Are you serious? Since I've been here, we've hung out with a load of tr—' He stops himself. '*Homeless people*, and then you went and lay down behind a supermarket with your sister. Clearly, you've got your own thing going on and you don't need me.'

I laugh. 'Well, now maybe you know how I feel.'

'What do you mean?' he says, folding his arms.

'You never text me back any more,' I say. 'Or if you

do, it's just one word.'

Ross rolls his eyes like I'm his annoying little brother. 'I'm just busy that's all.'

'Busy with all your new mates?' I snap back.

'Yeah, actually.' He stands up. 'And what's wrong with that? Did you expect me to just sit in a dark room on my own all the time? It's not my fault you went off and—'

'Got cancer?' I cut in.

Ross opens his mouth, then closes it again. I can tell he doesn't know what to say. Neither do I.

'You can send me to the gulags, but the spirit of the Soup Movement will live on!' The tension is burst by the sight of Abi being bundled out from behind Safebuys. For a second, it looks like she's going to get arrested, but then the policeman lets her go on the condition that she stays away from the premises.

'I won't need to come back,' says Abi. 'The world has seen what this place is about. Safebuys will be shut down within a month!'

At one time, I'd think that was a crazy thing to say. These days, I'm not so sure.

CHAPTER 12

Firework displays are supposed to be fun for all the family. Which is why it's an interesting experience to go to one when you're feeling completely miserable. After we came home from our filming/protest, we sat in silence. I let Ross play on the Xbox while I did homework. If he thinks I'm some kind of nerd, I might as well play up to it.

'Now, remember,' says Mum, cracking open a pack of mints as we walk into the park. 'You aren't to stand too close to the display. You never know if one of those rocket things is going to zoom off in the wrong direction. And stay off the rides. Those things are death traps. That goes for you too, Ross. I want to send you back to your parents in one piece, thank you very much.'

There's a fair, with waltzers and a little rollercoaster, and some kind of massive centrifuge thing in the place where Harry's tent normally stands. I wonder where he is.

'And one more thing,' says Mum. 'Don't eat anything from these stalls. Lord only knows what their hygiene rating is. You could go there for a burger and come away with salmonella.'

'But besides all that, have fun,' says Dad, winking and pressing a tenner into my hand.

I whisper a thanks, but I just want to stay home. How am I supposed to pass three hours in silence with Ross? Abi got out of coming by telling Mum and Dad she was busy revising, but really she was dealing with the fallout from the supermarket incident. When we left to come here, #BoycottSafebuys was trending all across the country. She had more journalists messaging her, wanting to get a quote. I could tell she was loving the attention. She's welcome to it, too.

'I'll meet you back here after the fireworks,' says Ross, the first time he'd spoken to me since our argument outside Safebuys.

'What are you on about?' I ask, but Ross is already walking away.

'I'm sure you've already got plans,' he says. 'And if they're anything like what you were doing earlier,

I'd rather not be involved.'

'Fine,' I say, in that Abi way, where it's pretty obvious I'm not fine. 'See you later.'

Ross nods, stuffs his hands in his pockets and leaves. Great. What am I supposed to do now? I can't go back to Mum and Dad, because they'll be asking where Ross is. Besides, I can see from here, they've gone to the bar and I'm probably not even allowed in there. I look around, at the candy-striped stalls selling rock-hard sugar dummies and sticky candy floss; at the baby rides with the same kind of dodgy knock-off Disney characters that were on the walls of the children's ward. This must all seem so lame to Ross. I'm not surprised he wants to go home.

Without even thinking about it, I hand Dad's tenner over to a Hook-a-Duck man. He gives me my seven quid change and my hook and it doesn't take me long to grab a plastic yellow duck from the water. The man pulls a big stuffed teddy down from the ceiling.

'You hooked a red-bottomed one,' he says. 'Top prize!'

Lucky me, I think.

As I walk away, a kid that looks about three years old is screaming. 'I want a toy!' over and over. His mum, who looks like she just wants to go to bed, tries to calm him down, but he's having none of it. I go over and give him the teddy, walking away before the mum can properly thank me.

Maybe I should try and find out where Harry's gone. I squeeze through the crowds and leave the park for a look around the town. I'm in no hurry to get back. There's something a bit sad about walking around a fair by yourself. The streets are dark, all shuttered shops and shadowy alleys. There's the occasional burst of light and chatter from old-man pubs, but other than that, it's deadly quiet. A ghost town. Maybe Abi's got a point.

When I get back, I head to the outer reaches of the park. To the dark areas Mum would hate me wandering around in. It doesn't take me long to find the tent, pitched in the shadows beneath an oak tree. I see little flickers of light behind it. They look like fireflies: tiny, orange sparks dancing on the breeze. It must be Harry messing with matches or something like that.

'Harry!'

I head around the back.

'Wait, you're not Harry.'

Will shoots a look at me. He's sitting in the grass

with a lighter in one hand and strips of paper in the other. His face looks puffy.

'What are you doing?' I ask him.

He says nothing, just lights up another strip and flicks it at the tent. It lands on the side and leaves a black burn mark.

'Hey, don't do that,' I say.

'Or what?' His voice is flat and emotionless.

I don't have an answer for that.

'This tent is all Harry has in the world,' I say to him. 'Why don't you just leave him alone?'

Will laughs and lights another strip. 'Harry, is he? On first name terms with the tramps, I see.' He flicks the strip, but I knock it off with my sleeve and grind it into the ground.

'It doesn't make you better than me, you know,' says Will. 'All this soup stuff.'

I wince. I knew he'd find out about it eventually. I just didn't realize it would be that fast.

'You come here from the city, thinking you're better than me, and you try to steal my friends.' He shakes his head. 'Nah. I'm not going to let that happen.'

'What are you talking about?' I cry. 'I'm not stealing your friends!

'Too right you're not,' he says, getting up and unzipping the tent. 'And I'm going to make sure your homeless mates know they're not welcome here, either.'

He flicks on the lighter and throws it into the tent. I dive in after it, but luckily, the flame is out. I pick up the lighter, leap out of the tent and throw it as hard as I can into the thick woods.

Will shoves me.

'What are you doing?' I yell. 'Leave me alone!'

'Nope,' he says, shoving me again. I flail back at him, but he dives backwards, then hits me with another shove. I try to get away, but he seems to be everywhere, quick as a cat. I'm dizzy and confused. Before I know what's happening, I'm stumbling backwards and I'm flat on my back. Somewhere high above us are three Chinese lanterns hovering like UFOs.

Will kneels over me, pinning my arms down. How is he so strong?

'Get off me! What's wrong with you?'

Will laughs. 'You don't want to know what's wrong with me, Jordan.'

I try my hardest to roll over, but he has me held down too firmly. I kick like crazy but I can't reach him.

'Oi, get off him!' I hear a voice approach. Thank God.

'Who are you?' says Will.

'I'm his mate. Now do one.'

It's Ross!

'What if I'm comfortable here?' says Will.

Next thing I know, I feel him launching off me and see him fly through the air and land on his back. I can only assume Ross has hit him with some kind of judo throw. I scramble to my feet and watch as Ross stands over Will, fists clenched.

'I'm not from round here,' he says. 'But if I find out you've been bothering Jordan again, I will come straight back and I will track you down. Do you get me?'

Ross sounds so hard and threatening. I've never heard him like that before.

'Whatever,' says Will, scrambling to his feet and walking away.

Ross nods at me. 'You OK?'

'Think so,' I say.

Ross walks over and picks a twig off my shoulder. 'Who was that psycho?'

'Some kid from school.'

Ross raises an eyebrow at me. 'It can't be easy

starting at a new place. I get it.'

I don't know what to say. At least he finally understands what I'm going through.

He holds out his hand. 'Sorry, man. We still mates?'

I shake it. 'Yeah. Always.'

Ross smiles. He's changed, but not that much. 'Come on,' he says. 'Don't want to miss these amazing fireworks, do we?'

We walk back towards the crowds, and I smile and try not to think about the yawning ache in my stomach as I wish things could be like they were before I got sick.

The fair is quiet now and everyone is gathered at the big, flat part of the park. There must be thousands of people here, practically the whole town. I remember this one New Year's Eve when we all went down to the Embankment to watch the fireworks. It was great and everything, but it took hours to get home and Abi moaned the entire time, which kind of ruined it.

When the first Pondstead Day fireworks start, I'm surprised at how good they are. I was expecting a few farty rockets, but this is actually quite impressive. They're all cued up with the music and when they explode, they spread across the entire night sky. Everyone goes 'ooh' and 'ahhh'. It's weirdly relaxing after being attacked by Will.

But wait a second. I recognize this song. Oh.

'Are you alright, Jordan?'

It's happened again, hasn't it? I've started crying without any warning whatsoever.

Ross jabs my arm awkwardly. 'Don't get upset about that idiot, man. He's not worth it.'

I nod and let him think it's Will that's made me cry and not the fact that the speakers are blasting that old Duran Duran song, 'Rio'. The one she hated.

I'm relieved when the fireworks intensify and get louder and faster because it drowns out the song. It's crazy how music can take you right back somewhere in an instant.

I see the crowds parting ahead of us. People look freaked out. Mums and Dads pull their kids close.

'Come away, he's mad,' I hear someone shout.

Who are they talking about? I see the shadow lumbering towards us, its hands clamped over its ears. An enormous banger goes off, lighting up the entire park. It's Harry. What's he doing?

'Under fire!' he screams. 'We need air support, now!'

He falls to his knees and presses his forehead into the cold ground in front of me.

'Harry!' I put my hand on his back, and he's shaking.

'Do you know him?' An event steward has arrived on the scene.

'Yes,' I say. 'Can you help me get him somewhere quieter?'

'Is he drunk?' the steward asks.

'No!' I say. 'He's just . . . I don't know what's wrong with him.'

The steward says something into his radio, and a minute later another steward arrives. Between the two of them, they drag Harry away from the display and put him on a bench. Me and Ross sit next to him.

'You need us to call the police?' one of them asks.

'Nah,' Ross replies. 'It's alright. He's my brother.'

I mouth 'thanks' at him, but he waves me off.

The fireworks display comes to an end and the crowds begin to file away. It won't be long before Mum comes looking for us.

Harry is sitting with his head in his hands,

shaking. When he finally looks up, his eyes are glazed. 'What happened?'

'You seemed like you were freaking out a bit, mate,' I say.

Harry growled and slapped his forehead. 'I thought I was better now.'

'Better?'

'You wouldn't understand,' he says. 'You're just a kid.'

'I might,' I say.

Harry looks at me. 'The war is over for me, in the real world,' he says. 'But up here.' He taps his temple with two fingers. 'It's still going on.'

I think about the 'Rio' song and my automatic tears. I think about my hospital nightmares with the shadow people.

'Yes,' I say. 'I know exactly what you mean.'

I exchange a quick look with Ross. I'm not sure, but he looks like he's finally realized something. Something he's been thinking about for ages but was unable to work out until now.

'I think I get it too,' he says.

We pooled together our resources and came up with the grand total of three pounds and sixty-two pence.

'He'll appreciate it,' said Rio. 'And if nothing else, it'll make him realize that someone cares. That's the main thing.'

'If you say so.'

Rio opened the rec room door slowly, knowing that to pull it any quicker would cause a massive creak and looked down the corridor towards the main door.

'OK,' she whispered to me. 'Kate's on her break and Pravina is busy at Bay Twelve. That just leaves Yolanda at the nurses' station.'

The nurses' station is a little way up the hall, towards the main doors. There's no sneaking past it without being seen.

'I reckon we've got five minutes until Kate comes back,' said Rio. 'So we need to activate phase one immediately.'

I gave her a brisk nod, then squeezed past out onto the corridor. Stepping as lightly as I could, I ran over to the bed opposite me, where a kid called Alex was dozing peacefully, and pressed his button. When I heard the alarm sound at the nurses' station, I ran back to the rec room and took cover, while Rio kept watch by the window.

After a minute, Yolanda hurried past the rec room to Alex's bed to see what he wanted. As soon as she got there, she'd see he's asleep, so we didn't have much time.

'Go, go, go,' Rio whispered, and we hurried along the corridor towards the main door. If Yolanda came back earlier than we thought, or Kate emerged from the break room, we'd be finished.

Rio mashed the green button which unlocked the door and I wrenched it open, holding it for Rio to make her escape before I followed.

The lifts stood to the left, and I quickly pressed the down button. When it arrived, the doors opening with an airy swish, I half expected to see Dr Kanelos or one of the nurses, or worse still, Mum in there, but thankfully, it was empty.

As we glided downwards, Rio sniffed the air. 'Smell

that?' she said.

'You haven't,' I said, disgusted.

'No,' she said. 'I meant the sweet smell of freedom.'

'Oh,' I said. 'Yeah. I suppose so.'

I glanced at our reflections in the mirrored back wall. We looked ridiculous, standing there in our pyjamas, Rio with a bucket hat on. But we decided that changing into our normal clothes would arouse too much suspicion, so it would have to be pyjamas.

Rio held out her hand, the change glistening under the energy-saving bulb above us. 'So we cross the road, drop the change in his bucket, bid him good day, then hurry back here.'

'Military precision.' I nod.

The lift doors opened to the main foyer, busy with people coming and going. The thick coffee smell from the café hit me and made me feel slightly sick, and the rows of magazines, sweets and crisps in the shop seemed too bright and vivid in the harsh sunlight that streamed in through the atrium.

'Game face on, Ollie,' said Rio. 'Don't stop, even for a second.'

We walked in a straight line, past rows of people sitting in the hard, metal seats, some looking worried, others simply bored, and headed for the automatic doors in front, which led to the ambulance bays and car park.

'Here we go,' said Rio, as we approached. 'Entering the big, wide world in five, four, three, two . . .'

We crossed the threshold and stood still for a moment, as if we'd just achieved something momentous. I felt like I do when I cheat to get to a restricted area in a computer game and suddenly get a five-star wanted level and police helicopters with mounted machine guns are hunting me down.

We crossed the car park and emerged onto the traffic-choked main road. Everything seemed too loud: a car revving at the lights, someone blasting old rock music, even a huddle of laughing men taking up the pavement as they walked towards us. I looked at Rio to see if she was as overwhelmed as I was, but if she was, it wasn't showing. She was determined to get this mission completed.

She pressed the button at the crossing and soon, the cars came to a stop, allowing us to cross. It was a hot day, and the sun burned the back of my neck. As we crossed, the busker came into clearer view, and I could hear him thrashing away at his bongos, his hair covering his face. No wonder he wasn't making much money, he sounded like a sack of coconuts falling down the stairs.

'Remember!' Rio yelled over the noise, reading my mind. 'It's not about the musicianship, it's about showing him that someone cares.'

Just as well. When we reached the other side of the road, a sickly feeling began to churn my stomach. This busker looked familiar. Very familiar. I tried to stop Rio, but she was too far ahead. She dropped the change into his bucket with a loud clatter. The busker stopped playing and flipped his lank brown hair out of his face. Oh, no.

'Thanks kids,' he said, with a big grin. 'Nice PJs.' His hazy eyes moved from Rio, to me, and they came alive with recognition.

'Jordan!' he cried. 'Fancy seeing you here, my dude. It's a drag to hear you're sick, man.'

I closed my eyes for a second. Since when did Abi's goofy friend, Leonard busk?

Before I could say anything, he got his phone out.

'Wait, what are you doing?' I said.

He held his phone up, as if he was FaceTiming. 'Hey Abs! Guess who I'm here with?'

Rio looked at me as if to say, 'WHAT IS GOING ON?'

'Please don't!' I yelled at Leonard, but he'd already

turned around and got me and Rio on screen. And I could see Abi.

'What the hell are you doing out of the ward, Jordan?' she said.

'We just wanted to bring him some money!' I said, kind of pathetically.

'You wanted to bring Leonard money?' Abi yelled. 'You know as well as I do his parents are worth a million quid.'

'Hey, I'm an independent man, following my dreams, babe,' said Leonard.

'Do not call me babe,' Abi snapped.

'We'll be off, then,' I said, but then I saw a shadow fall behind Abi and was frozen to the spot.

'Jordan Michael Turner, get back in that hospital this instant,' Mum yelled, making Abi wince.

'Oh, no,' I croaked.

Part of me thought it had all been worth it, because at least we got to do something different. Another, bigger part of me knew it wasn't worth it because Mum was on her way to the hospital and she was going to kill me to death.

BUZZ NEWS

THE WORLD IS GOING TO HELL!
OMG HEAD FOR YOUR NUCLEAR BUNKERS!

You'd be forgiven for saying any of the above if you've paid even the tiniest bit of attention to the news lately.

So we at Buzz News have decided to bring you some news that will add some spring to your step and show you that everything's not lost.

In the unassuming town of Pondstead, thirteen-year-old Jordan Turner is making a difference, by feeding the homeless.

His sister, up and coming influencer Abi xx, has been chronicling what has become known as the 'Soup Movement' and says her brother is an inspiration. And we can't help but agree.

To top it off, their protest outside Safebuys, the supermarket that calls the police on homeless people who take food from their bins, has created a huge social-media backlash, with many people vowing never to use the company again.

Young Jordan has reminded us that while big things around the world aren't going great, we can make a real difference on our doorstep. We salute you, Jordan!

CHAPTER
13

Ross's mum has just picked him up. It was weird seeing him again, but at least it feels like we understand each other at last.

Last night, when we got in, I did some googling and I think Harry might have something called Post Traumatic Stress Disorder, or PTSD. The website said PTSD is caused by frightening events. It says 'the affected person may relive the event through nightmares or flashbacks.' Man. Maybe I have it, too. I don't like the idea of having a 'disorder', but the more I read about it, the more I think, 'that's me.'

When Abi and I arrive at the loading bay, we find Elaine, Daniela and the Captain.

'Here they are, the protestors,' says Elaine, with a big smile.

'Safebuys are going to have to change, mark my

words,' says Abi. 'Right. Who wants to be interviewed next?'

My sister starts filming on her phone.

ABI: Hi guys, we're back, free from the interfering arm of the law and ready to take on the world. Today, we're talking to Daniela.

DANIELA: Hi.

ABI: So, tell us, Daniela, what's your story?

DANIELA: I am from Romania. A town called Arad. I grew up in care. It was . . . not good.

ABI: I'm sorry to hear that, Daniela. So how did you end up here?

DANIELA: I met a man. He told me he would help me come here, to make a new life. He told me he liked my drawings.

ABI: So you're an artist?

DANIELA: Yes!

She pulls papers out of her bag and holds them up to the camera. They are beautiful sketches of old buildings.

ME: They're amazing.

DANIELA: Thank you.

ME: So what happened? How come you're not a famous artist?

DANIELA: The man was a liar. He made me work for no money, picking potatoes. It was worse than the orphanage.

ABI: What a scumbag.

DANIELA: Yes. We would work more than twelve hours a day in all weather. We had very little to eat. One day, the guard stepped away for a minute, so I took the opportunity to run, and this is where I ended up. I still prefer it to the fields.

ABI: Oh my God. Daniela, that's awful.

Daniela shrugs and looks at the ground.

ME: If you don't mind, could you show the camera your drawings again, please?

Daniela holds up the pictures.

ABI: Good thinking, Jordan. OK, Internet. Do your

thing. We need to get this amazing young artist's work out there.

I leave Abi to carry on with filming and head over to the park. By now, the fair is pretty much gone, leaving huge square dents in the grass where the rides and stalls were. I see Harry in the middle of the field, pulling a wheelie bin around and picking up all the litter that's been left behind.

'Some people have no consideration,' he says to me, shaking his head.

He's right. How would I feel if a load of people left tons of rubbish in my back garden?

'Bit of a neat freak, as you might have guessed,' he says, picking up a crushed Coke can.

'Let me give you a hand,' I say, scooping up a carton of half-eaten fries and dropping it in the bin.

'Cheers,' he says, quietly, before stopping and leaning on the handle. 'Sorry about last night, by the way.'

I don't know what to say. He shouldn't have to apologize for how his brain works. It's not like he can help it.

Harry runs a hand down his face, which is more bristly than usual. 'I thought I had it under control.'

'Can I ask you something?' I say.

He nods.

'Do you have something called PTSD?'

For a minute he looks thrown; maybe he didn't expect me to know what PTSD is? But then he nods.

'The docs put me on a waiting list for therapy.' He chuckles bitterly. 'I'm sure I'll get the call any day now.' He hesitates. 'You know about PTSD?'

'Sort of,' I say.

Harry raises his eyebrows at me. 'Someone you know got it?'

'Not exactly.'

'What do you mean?' he asks. 'Have you got it?'

I swallow hard. 'No. Well, I don't know. I mean, I might.'

Harry's forehead creases into thick furrows. 'Did something bad happen to you?'

I hesitate for a second. I could lie and change the subject. But he's told me so much about himself, it would be very un-pinky swear not to do the same.

'Kind of,' I say. 'I had cancer.'

Harry whispers a swear word, then quickly apologizes. 'You're clear now, though?'

I nod.

'And you get nightmares?'

'Yes,' I say.

Harry sighs. 'Yeah, I know what that's like. I'm sorry you're going through it, kid. You're too young.'

I try to croak something about how it could always be worse, but a cricket ball-sized lump has appeared in my throat and I'm doing my best to swallow it. But before I can say anything else, I hear muffled shrieking coming from the other side of the park. The shrieking soon becomes clearer. And very familiar.

'There he is! Get away from that man immediately, Jordan.'

This time, I'm the one that swears.

To begin with, I can't believe that Mum is actually dragging Abi across the field. I think it must be some kind of hallucination.

'What's going on?' I ask.

'I'll tell you what's going on,' says Mum. 'I know what you two have been up to.' Her face is bright pink and she looks like a giant Peperami.

I glance at Abi, but she's just staring at the ground with a look of pure murder on her face.

'Yes, I've seen the videos. Lying on the floor and nearly getting arrested? I ask you!' Mum shakes her head. 'And, not to be unkind, but do you have any idea how many germs these people have on them?'

'You're aware I can hear you, right?' says Harry.

Mum looks at Harry for the first time. 'Stay away from my son!' she shrieks.

Harry raises his hands, a little smile on his face, but Mum doesn't see because OH MY GOD, SHE'S SLATHERING ME IN ANTI-BACTERIAL GEL.

'You know what bothers me the most?' she says, her voice wobbly. 'It's that you lied to me. You told me that soup was for your friends.'

'It was for my friends,' I say, trying to wriggle away from her slimy hands.

Mum groans. 'I mean friends your own age. Friends that don't live in a tent.'

'Oh my God, Mum, why are you so judgemental?' says Abi.

'That's enough from you,' she says, rounding on her. 'From both of you. From now on, you're grounded. You go to school and college and you come straight home. There will be no more consorting with vagrants.'

'You're mad,' Abi cries. 'And you're talking like a Victorian schoolmistress.'

Mum grips my arm so tight it hurts and drags me away from Harry. 'If wanting to protect your children is mad, then I am a raving lunatic. Now come on. We're going home.'

We sit in silence in the car, both me and Abi in the back. She pokes my leg and I turn to look at her.

'This isn't over,' she whispers, then pulls out her phone and starts tapping.

Abi's Instagram

 **abi_xx**

MESSAGE TO ALL FOLLOWERS OF THE SOUP MOVEMENT

Due to circumstances beyond our control, the Soup Movement has had to (temporarily) cease operations.

We are devastated about this setback and are determined to get back to work as quickly as possible.

But for now, we need your help. Keep pushing Safebuys to change their corporate policy and keep spreading the Soup Movement message. Together, we shall overcome!

Abi xx and Jordan.

CHAPTER 14

I could hardly sleep last night. And when I did, the nightmares came back. I dreamt that Mum had sealed me in an airtight bubble and the only contact I had with the outside world was a tube that pumped in soup three times a day. Then, as an extra special twist, I turned into a chicken. The nightmares don't always make sense.

When we got home yesterday, Mum made me take off all my clothes so she could wash them at the highest temperature. It didn't matter to her that Harry is actually very clean and probably has no more germs than anyone else.

She only found out about the Soup Movement when Auntie Denise saw it on Buzz News and sent her a text saying, 'You must be so proud.' And, I don't want to blow my own horn, but that's exactly what she should be. I'm honouring the pinky swear

137

and making this town she's forced us to live in a better place, and this is how she reacts? Like I've joined some kind of criminal gang?

I stew about it all morning at school. I didn't even notice Will wasn't in until the beginning of the last lesson before lunch. Which was Food Tech. Yep. Good old Miss Booker got us making onion bhajis. Delicious onion bhajis. I think I know four people who'd really like them. If I go wandering into town on my lunchbreak, and just happen to run into them, what's the harm in sharing some of my school work?

I place the eight bhajis into a plastic box and head out. If I hurry, they'll still be warm when I arrive. They don't look too bad, by my standards. They're a deep red with just a few hints of black. They smell good, too. It might not be soup, but it's better than nothing.

I round the corner at the top of the road and stop dead. No, she hasn't. Surely not. I jump back around the corner, and then peep out from behind the wall. I can't believe it. Mum is parked next to the loading bay. She's come to make sure I'm not bringing them anything. I take a walk around the block and come back, but she's still there.

I head back to school, trying to think of a way to

get around Mum, but drawing a blank. This is not good. Not good at all.

To: Abi xx
From: Abdul Rashid

Hi Abi and Jordan

My name is Abdul and I'm fourteen years old. I live in Glasgow.

When I saw your videos, it made me want to do something, so me and my friends have started our own Soup Movement. It's early days, but we've already managed to fced ten people!

Thanks for the inspiration and I hope you can get back up and running soon.

Abdul

To: Abi xx
From: Scarlett Rosenberg

Hi guys!

Just wanted you to know that I've started my own Soup Movement near my house in Liverpool. Me and my friend Cara take it in turns to make soup every day and we take it to the two ladies that live in the park.

We're changing the world!

Scarlett

HEAVEN SPELLED BACKWARDS

I didn't think I'd get that bad a telling off, what with me having cancer and everything, but I was dead wrong. Mum arrived at the hospital within half an hour of my escape and chewed me up like a piece of beef. Honestly. I tried explaining that we were just trying to do a nice thing and help out the busker, but she streamrolled my every attempt. She even tried to get me moved to a different bed, to get me away from Rio's 'bad influence', but Kate calmed her down, made her a cup of tea and eventually got her to drop the idea.

To top it all off, the following day, I started my next round of chemo. Mum, of course, didn't leave my side even for a second. Like, where was I going to go hooked up to an IV? Come on.

My treatment sucks. I don't know how many days went by before I felt normal again. I thought I might have got used to chemo by now, but no, my guts still go into reject mode every time. Rio helped, reminding me about my breathing techniques, even though I could tell Mum wanted her to go away.

The other day, though, I woke up feeling, well, good. Or if not good, something in the same neighbourhood. I didn't ache or throb or feel like my stomach had been taken out and replaced with a spinning ball of molten lava. When Kate brought me a bowl of soggy cornflakes, I actually was a bit excited to eat them. I know that sounds like the saddest thing in the world, but when your entire world is reduced to one room, little things seem huge.

And. Big news. We've got a new resident in our end. Gregory, the little boy opposite me who was in having his tonsils out has gone home, and has been replaced by Nevaeh. She's about fourteen, I'd say, and she's in after having an operation on her eye. Well, I think that's what it is. She's got a big patch on.

Looking up from writing yesterday, I noticed her looking at me. I carried on writing for a while and when I glanced up, she was still looking right at me. I gave her a smile, one of those thin half-smiles that makes you look like you've got wind.

'Hello,' she said.

'Hi.'

'Your name's Jordan, right?' It's handy having your name written on a board behind your head. Really gets you past that awkward introduction stage.

'I'm Nevaeh,' she said—which was a relief because I had no idea how to pronounce it—Nev-ay-ah.

'Weird name, I know,' she went on. 'It's heaven spelled backwards.'

Oh yeah, so it is. I wish my name spelled something backwards. Nadroj? What's that?

'Can you do me a favour, Jordan?' she asked. 'I'm supposed to be reading this book for English but with one eye not working, it's a nightmare. Could you read it for me? I've only got a few pages left.'

'Um, OK,' I said.

I went over and sat in the chair next to her bed. She had a stack of four books on her table, next to half a glass of orange squash.

'It's the top one,' she said. 'I've been trying to read it but it's giving me a headache.'

'Oh,' I say, holding up her copy of A Midsummer Night's Dream. 'I'm reading this, too!'

'Yeah?' Nevaeh replied. 'What do you think of it?'

I shrugged. 'Not a big fan, to be honest.'

'Really?' she sat up. 'I think it's magical. I watched

a film version and it helped me to understand it better. I've got it on my iPad if you want to watch it later.'

'That'd be brilliant,' I replied. 'I mean, they're not being that strict with me about schoolwork, but I don't want to get too far behind.'

'Are you in for a long time, then?'

I nodded. 'Yeah, chemo takes ages.'

'Oh.' She narrowed her eye at me and pushed her long hair back. 'I'm sorry. You don't have to read that if you're not feeling up to it.'

'No, it's fine,' I said. 'I'm actually feeling OK today. Besides, this will help me with my stupid homework.'

I opened the book at the marked page and started reading. She was a bit ahead of me. Titania was in the middle of a speech. I wasn't completely sure what she was talking about and I was inwardly panicking that I was saying it all wrong, but Nevaeh wasn't complaining, at least.

I'd been reading for about five minutes when Rio came back and got into bed. Even looking at the book, I could sense her glaring at me. I picked up the pace and rushed to the end. Turns out it's hard to recite Shakespeare in a hurry.

'That was brilliant,' said Nevaeh. 'Thanks very much, Jordan.'

'That's alright,' I said, knowing that Rio was eyeballing me. 'Anyway, I'd better be . . .' I stopped and pointed at my bed.

Nevaeh gave me a thumbs up. 'Thanks again.'

I climbed back into bed and looked at Rio. She picked up her tablet and turned her back on me. She didn't speak to me for the rest of the day. Both our parents came and went, we had dinner, (chilli con carne. Again) and still nothing. Every time I tried to make conversation, she'd shut me down. Nevaeh was pretty chatty though. We talked about books a lot, and she recommended some I should check out when I leave. Whenever *that* is. We do have a little library here, but there's not much selection. Maybe I'll ask Mum to pick me some up and bring them in. Honestly, with how slow the days go by here, I'd read the back of a cereal packet for entertainment.

'Hey, Jordan. I've got that *Midsummer Night's Dream* film on here, if you want to come over and watch?' said Nevaeh today.

I sneaked a look at Rio, glaring at her tablet, probably making a playlist of the most angry songs in the world. Her eyes snapped onto mine. 'Don't feel like you have to stay here on my account,' she said, frostily. 'Go over there and play Shakespeare with your new best friend.'

'I'm sorry,' said Nevaeh. 'I didn't realize I was causing a problem. You can come over, too, if you'd like.'

Rio laughed without smiling. 'No thanks. I'd hate to be a third wheel. Besides, I try not to get too close to Jordan. I hear fleas can jump.'

Neveah's only good eye widened, while all the blood in my body rushed to my face. 'I do not have fleas!' I cried.

'You're among friends here, Jordan,' said Rio, her gaze steely. 'You don't have to be ashamed of your fleas. Or your bed wetting.'

'I DO NOT WET THE BED!'

Rio gave Nevaeh a tight smile and whispered, 'I see them changing his sheets every morning, Nivea. It's not a pretty sight.'

Nevaeh ignored Rio, luckily able to tell what was happening, and looked at me. 'So are you coming over?'

I got straight out of bed and went over. If Rio was going to be horrible, I didn't want to be next to her anyway.

I sat in the chair, but Nevaeh shifted over and patted the edge of her bed. 'No, you can perch on here.

Then we'll both be able to see it.'

I heard Rio growl from the other side of the room but kept my eyes on the screen.

Nevaeh was right. Watching it did make it easier to understand. I even got some of the jokes. When I read it was supposed to be a comedy, I thought it must have been a typo, but seeing the actors perform the words on the page really got it across. I also thought the idea of fairies controlling people was pretty interesting. Imagine if that was real. My fairy must have a real sick sense of humour. 'I'M GONNA GIVE HIM CANCER AND MAKE HIM HALF BALD LOL!'

It was beginning to get dark and I sensed Rio's tablet being switched off in my outer vision. Then she got out of bed and heavily stomped past us, into the corridor, shooting us evils on the way.

I excused myself to Nevaeh and followed Rio into the rec room where she stood staring out of the window. The streets below were full of cars with headlights on. People coming home from work or going shopping. Normal life going on while in here we're stuck in suspended animation like Captain America.

'Rio?'

She looked at me sideways in pretend shock. 'Oh, who is this stranger?'

'Why are you being like this?'

Rio's laugh had fogged up the glass and she started drawing the outline of a house in it with her finger. 'Being like what? I'm *fine*.'

I let out a long breath. An ambulance was pulling into the bay, blue lights twinkling. Looked like another new arrival.

'You're not fine though, are you?'

'Course I am. Don't worry about me. Just carry on hanging out with your girlfriend, Never.'

My face burned. 'She is not my girlfriend. And it's pronounced Nev-ey-ah. It's heaven spelled backwards.'

Rio laughed bitterly. 'You know what my name spelled backwards is? Oir. As in 'Oi, R you taking the mick?'

'Oh my God, Rio, she asked me to read to her because she's only got one good eye. The only reason I agreed was because I thought it was a mitzvah. You know, the thing we pinky swore to do at every opportunity? Walking by is FORBIDDEN? I thought the pinky swear was sacrosanct.'

Rio spun around and looked at me properly for the first time. She had dark rings under her eyes. 'Wrong. It's not a mitzvah if you're going to get something out of it.'

'What am I getting out of it?'

'Plenty,' she almost shouted. 'When the two of you get out of here, I bet you'll be best of friends and you'll forget all about me.'

'You're being ridiculous,' I said. 'I mean, you're getting out of here one day, too. Who's to say we're not going to be best friends?'

Her chin wobbled a little and she rubbed her eyes with the back of her hand. 'Yeah, yeah I know I'm getting out one day. But look at me and look at her. She's got gorgeous long, blonde hair and a lovely smile and I look like an exhausted cue ball. Beautiful people always win.'

'But Rio, I—'

'Leave me alone, Jordan,' she said.

'Rio—'

'I said, LEAVE ME ALONE.' And with that, she turned her back on me and stared out of the window again.

Ugh. Why is everything so hard?

CHAPTER
15

We've never had a 'family meeting' before. I'm not even sure what a family meeting is. All I know is, we're having one any minute now. Dad says we have to. Abi and Mum were having a screaming row in the kitchen when I got in from school. Abi said she was going on hunger strike until Mum stopped interfering with the Soup Movement.

Mum said she was being ridiculous, and Abi asked if I'd join her on the strike. I said yes, even if the idea makes me feel a bit sick. That was when Mum got on the phone to Dad at work.

So, now the three of us are sitting around the table in silence. Dad's running late. God, I'm famished. This hunger strike is only two hours old and it's killing me already.

The room is silent except for Mum clacking a mint around in her mouth. She's on her second pack of the afternoon. Abi looks up from her phone and tuts.

'Less of the attitude,' Mum snaps.

Ding! Round two!

'Deal,' says Abi. 'I'll stop with the so-called attitude as soon as you stop being such an obstructionist.'

'Oh, why can't you be a normal teenager?' Mum snaps. 'When I was your age, I was going to concerts with my friends not—'

'Helping people?' Abi cuts in. 'Caring? And anyway, maybe I would still go out with my friends if you hadn't forced me to move away from them.'

Mum's face tightens as if someone has cranked a bolt on the back of her head. 'You are impossible,' she hisses.

'And you are on the wrong side of history,' says Abi, slapping the table. 'Did you know Soup Movements have already started in Glasgow and Liverpool? We are unstoppable.'

I can't help but feel my chest swell with pride when she puts it like that. Maybe we've started something really amazing.

The front door opens and the unmistakable smell of fish and chips wafts in.

'Stay strong,' Abi whispers to me. 'Don't let them win with psychological warfare.'

Dad walks in, throws his car keys on the counter and plonks a big paper bag in the middle of the table. Abi closes her eyes and I see a little smile on Mum's face. They probably planned this. Get the most delicious smelling food to break the hunger strike.

Dad sits down and smiles at me. His eyes are tired but he looks happy.

'Alright, kiddywinkles,' he says, tearing open the bag. 'The strike is over.'

'It is not,' Abi huffs, folding her arms.

'Yes it is,' says Dad, passing her over a polystyrene box.

'You underestimate my resolve, Father Dear,' says Abi. 'As long as the homeless people go hungry, so shall we.'

Dad passes my box over. I can tell without opening it that's it's a mini fish and chips special with mushy peas. My favourite.

'The strike,' Dad says again. 'Is over.'

'This kind of treatment contravenes the Geneva Convention,' says Abi. 'I've looked it up.'

Dad chuckles as he passes Mum's box to her, then opens his own and takes a big bite from his sausage. 'There's no need to call the UN just yet,' he says. 'The reason the strike is over is because as of tomorrow the Soup Movement is back on.'

'What?' Mum shrieks.

Dad takes another bite of saveloy and nods appreciatively. 'This is so good.'

'What are you talking about, Graham? We're supposed to be putting on a united front,' says Mum.

Dad shifts in his seat and pulls out his phone. 'You remember my mate, Steve? Works at *The Times*?'

'Yes?' says Mum, looking more confused by the second.

'Well, he emailed me earlier with a tip-off.'

Abi's phone buzzes and she checks it. After a second, a huge smile spreads across her face. 'Oh my God.'

Dad nods. 'And now it looks like the news is officially breaking. Why not read it out, Abi?'

BUZZ NEWS

SAFEWAY BUCKLES

We told you we were going to start bringing you some sunnier news and we weren't lying.

That's right, everyone's favourite young crusaders have done it again, this time, forcing the hand of one of the country's biggest supermarkets.

After days of #BoycottSafebuys affecting their profit margins, Safebuys' CEO, Henry Foxton, has today announced that they will start handing out unsold food to homeless people.

'We have listened to the public and they're telling us loud and clear that they want us to change.' Foxton told a press conference.

But that's not all. Foxton also announced that they will support the Pondstead Soup Movement by donating ingredients to their cause. Exciting or what?

We'll be keeping our eyes on these guys. If they can sort out a supermarket in a week, they'll probably have global hunger licked within the month.

'Wow!' I say.

'Wow indeed,' says Dad. 'So it seems that the Soup Movement continues whether you like it or not.'

Mum's hands shake as she folds the mint wrapper. 'Doesn't matter,' she says. 'I won't allow you to use my kitchen to make it.'

I don't understand her. Isn't she at least a tiny bit impressed at what we've achieved? She must be, somewhere, deep down.

Abi laughs. 'We'll sort something out. You can't stop this, Mum, so you might as well get on board.'

Mum goes to get up, but then sits back down and turns to Dad. 'Why are you taking their side?'

Dad laughs. 'Claire, we are living the dream. Our two kids are out there feeding the homeless, and inspiring others to do the same! Would you rather them be shoplifting?'

'No,' says Mum, her chin trembling. 'I'd rather them be safe.'

Dad sighs and puts down the remains of his saveloy. Then he reaches over and holds Mum's hand. 'I get it,' he says. 'What happened . . .' He smiles at me. 'It's affected us all. How could it not? But here's the thing.' His Adam's apple bobs. 'We can't keep Jordan in a bubble for the rest of our lives.'

My eyes snap to his. He can't know about my nightmares, can he? That's impossible!

Mum looks stunned. 'But he's hanging around with random homeless people! They could be dangerous!'

'Understood,' says Dad, turning to me. 'So there's a new rule. You're not to meet anyone on your own. That sound reasonable?'

I nod.

Abi chuckles bitterly. 'Typical. Precious Jordan has to be safe, but I could go on a camping holiday with a coachload of serial killers and you wouldn't be bothered.'

Dad laughs and puts his arm around Abi. 'So there we go. I believe that's what we call a compromise.'

Mum takes a deep breath and blinks slowly.

'We've done a great job at this parenting lark, darling,' says Dad.

Mum looks at me, and for the first time I notice the lines around her eyes. They weren't there before I got sick. It's as if my cancer has drawn energy and life out of her. I get out of my chair, walk over and give her a hug. I feel her crying into my chest, and it sends an ice-cold shiver up my spine.

I used to think that cancer was a thing that just happened to one person, and when it's gone, it's gone. But it's not. It's like a weed growing in the garden, intertwining its roots into the plants all around it and choking them.

Cancer sucks.

CHAPTER
16

I arrive at school to find Mr Grimshaw waiting for me. He fixes me with a big smile and a peace sign. Grimshaw isn't a typical head teacher. He's probably about my grandad's age, with long white hair pulled back into a ponytail and a pair of Jesus sandals on. He wears a suit, but he looks like he'd be more at home in a tatty T-shirt and ripped jeans.

'Hey, Jordan,' he says. 'Step into my office for a sec. Promise you're not in trouble.'

He leads me through a door, closing it behind him. He has an incense stick burning on his windowsill, and a huge painting of a skeleton with roses on its head and the words 'The Grateful Dead' above it. I've never been in here before, yet it's pretty much exactly what I expected.

Grimshaw motions for me to have a seat and plonks himself down opposite.

'So,' he says, still smiling. 'You've made quite the splash since you arrived here. And, let me tell you, I think that's groovy.'

I don't know what to say. This is the first time I've ever spoken to him. In fact, the only time I've really heard him speak was when he gave an assembly on how we shouldn't bully each other because we're all connected by 'cosmic vibrations'.

'Oh, thanks,' I say.

'Now, I'm not going to insult your intelligence; the school has had a lot of good press, thanks to the Soup Movement, but that doesn't exactly sit right with me.'

'Oh?'

Grimshaw scratches his beard thoughtfully. 'I'm an old-fashioned sort of guy, in case you hadn't noticed.'

My eye drifts to a poster that says 'Glastonbury Festival: 1978.'

'Not really,' I say.

'Well, what I'm trying to say is, I don't like taking credit for stuff when I haven't put the work in.' He stops and narrows his eyes, like he's thinking of what to say next. 'So I was wondering how we could be of assistance.'

I think about it for a second. My first instinct is to come up with some excuse. It's hard enough to organize things with Abi making her YouTube videos without getting Mr Grimshaw involved. But then I remember, I don't have any actual soup now, because Mum can't bring herself to carry on making it. And what is a Soup Movement without soup?

'Actually, we're having some, uh, trouble with the kitchen at the moment,' I say.

Grimshaw holds up his hands. 'Say no more. I'll see to it that you can have use of one of the food classrooms. We've got state-of-the-art gear in there. You could pan fry a goat in five minutes, no problem. Not that I'd recommend that, of course.'

'Oh, wow, thanks,' I say.

'Don't sweat it,' says Grimshaw. 'I've got to admit, this kind of grassroots activism reminds me of the old days, blockading the animal testing plant with all my brothers and sisters.' He leans back and gazes at the ceiling, a big smile on his face. 'Real good times.'

I'm considering clearing my throat or shaking him when he finally comes around.

'Tell you what else we could do,' he goes on. 'We could put out a call for volunteers. Work up a rota and have fresh batches cooked up every lunchtime. It'll be a real production line for you.'

'That sounds good,' I say, relieved that I won't have to do all the soup-making myself.

I thank Grimshaw again and he stands up with a smile and shakes my hand. 'Stick it to the Man, son,' he says. 'Stick it to the Man.'

CHAPTER
17

Day one of the Soup Movement making its big move into school. I have a quick sandwich before heading up to Miss Booker's kitchen, but when I get there, I find it empty. Huh. Mr Grimshaw's drive for volunteers must not be going well so far.

I find a crate of vegetables with a Safebuys logo on the side. We organized to have the ingredients delivered straight here. There's potatoes and leeks and peas and carrots and corn on the cob, along with a full spice rack and a note to say the meat is in the fridge. It's only now, looking at all this, that I realize that I have no idea how to make soup. Not a clue.

Come on, Jordan, think about it. What is soup but a load of stuff bunged in a pan and cooked for a bit? How hard could it be? I google 'soup recipes' and find one I can use. 'Granny's veggie soup.'

I gather together a bottle of olive oil, a carrot, a

potato, a garlic clove, some tomatoes, cauliflower, celery, vegetable stock and Worcester sauce. I chop all of the veg into little pieces then I pour a load of oil into a pan and turn on the hob, before adding the carrots, potatoes and garlic as directed by the website. While it cooks, I go back to the board and chop the celery up even smaller in the hope that it will lessen its disgusting taste. I reckon even if I was homeless and starving, I'd still turn down celery.

I head back to the hob but nothing is happening. The veg is just sitting in a puddle of oil, going soggy. What's going on? Ah. I've put the wrong hob on.

I put the right one on and watch as the oil slowly starts to bubble. Should it do that? I go back to the recipe and see it recommends 'a splash' of oil. Mine is more a tidal wave than a splash. Great. I'm trying to help them and I'm going to end up poisoning them to death.

The door opens and Mr Grimshaw strides in wearing an apron with 'Vegan Superhero' on it. 'How's it going?'

I don't have to answer. The puddle of oily, mushy veg does all the talking for me.

'This is perfectly salvageable,' he says, not sounding totally convincing. 'We'll just . . .' He pokes at the veg with a wooden spoon and grimaces. 'Let's put this down as a first draft, eh?'

Grimshaw grabs a load of veg out of the box and starts chopping, directing me to help. 'I used to make this for our peace camps outside the Air Force base,' he says. 'It gives you all the energy you need for starting a revolution.'

When it's done, I ladle it into four flasks. Mr Grimshaw says I'm allowed to be late for the first lesson after lunch. At least until we've sorted more volunteers.

When I get to the loading bay, Abi is already there. I biked as quickly as I could to get them delivered before I have to go back to school, and now I feel like all the air has been squeezed out of my lungs and replaced with sand.

'You're here just in time for my interview with Elaine,' she says.

'Well, you sorted Safebuys for us, so I had to keep to my word,' Elaine says, with a shrug.

I hand the flasks out to the others, then stand by and watch.

ABI: Hey guys, Abi xx here. Today, I'm talking to Elaine.

ELAINE: Hello!

ABI: So you said you'd only talk to us if we made Safebuys change their ways, et voila! Here we are.

ELAINE: Yeah, fair play to you. To be honest, I didn't think you'd pull it off.

ABI: Never doubt the power of the Soup Movement, Elaine. So, while we're here, why don't you tell us your story?

ELAINE (Goes to speak, then stops): Actually, can I have a minute?

Abi turns the camera off and asks if Elaine is OK.

Elaine nods. 'Yeah, I'll be fine. I just.' She takes a deep breath. 'Need a sec.'

'Soup boy!' The Captain waves his flask at me.

'Yes?'

'This soup's rubbish!'

I look to Harry for reassurance but he grimaces. 'It's alright, mate,' he says. 'Did your mum switch up the recipe or something?'

'Well, Mum doesn't make it anymore, so Mr

164

Grimshaw from school did it,' I say.

'Send it back!' says the Captain.

Elaine takes a deep breath then nods. 'OK, I'm ready.'

ELAINE: Here's the thing. I don't want to talk about how I got here. It's too much for me. It ain't fair how I got here, but you know what? Life ain't fair. But I've got something I want the people watching this to know about, if that's OK?

ABI: Of course.

ELAINE: We're human beings. The people you see on the streets. We're living, breathing humans, just like you. You don't have to avoid us. You don't have to be scared. I don't expect everyone to give me change as they go by, but a little smile or a nod would be nice. Just something to make me feel like I exist. It goes a long way. That's why this Soup what-do-you-call-it thing is so good. It's more than just soup.

ABI: Thank you, Elaine. I'm glad you were able to speak to us.

THE
HOSPITAL BLOG

SOZ

The consultant, Dr Kanelos came around today while I was hooked up to the drip. He said I'm responding well to the treatment. I mean, it doesn't feel like I am. I still feel like I've been scraped off the bottom of a hippo's hoof. Wait, do hippos even have hooves?

Nevaeh went home today. She came over and said goodbye. I couldn't do much, what with being stuck in bed, but still. Abi was annoying, too. All, 'Ooh, was that your girlfriend?' I glanced at Rio, but she had her earphones in, frowning at her tablet. She hasn't spoken to me since two nights ago, when she went off on one in the rec room.

I'm just about over the puking phase now. Always a relief to get that out of the way. I managed to eat a hard-boiled egg and some spinach for lunch and keep it down. I'm becoming a pro at this. Mum and Abi had to leave not long after that because it's Abi's sixth form parents' evening. I miss stuff like that. Normal stuff. Parents' evenings, reports. Being in here is like living on the International Space Station, Rio says. Like, you get updates about Earth, but you can only watch from a distance. Hold on a sec, I've been bluetoothed something.

Huh. It was from Rio. It was a blank page with 'soz' written on it. I looked over at her, but she just stared at her tablet. I downloaded the picture and added 'That's OK' to it before sending it back. Now she's replied with 'rec room?' added to it.

She got out of bed and headed out into the corridor. I suppose I should go with her.

OK, I'm back in bed. It's been quite a night. Wow.

When I went into the rec room, Rio was putting a DVD into the player. 'Want to watch?'

I took the seat on the sofa next to her. She tucked her knees up under her chin and wrapped her arms around her legs, her eyes never leaving the screen. When the DVD finally started properly, I saw what it was: A Midsummer Night's Dream.

'I got my mum to bring it,' she said.

'Oh,' I said. 'Thank you.'

Rio thumped my arm lightly. 'Sorry for going mad

the other day. Wasn't very mitzvah-y of me, I know.'

'It's fine,' I said. 'You've more than made up for it.'

Rio smiled and I felt her relax a little. It was a different version of the film to the one I watched with Nevaeh but I found myself getting into it just the same. Rio asked a few questions, wanting to know who was who, but it wasn't annoying, not like when my nan does it all the way through *Black Panther*.

The way old Willy Shakespeare put the story together was really clever, having all these different characters plotting and scheming behind each other's backs.

Somehow, due to Oberon, king of the fairies, getting all devious, his wife Titania ends up falling in love with Bottom (lol), despite the fact that he has the head of an ass (double lol) and she gets dead affectionate with him, kissing him all over his donkey face.

'Gross,' said Rio.

'I don't know,' I said. 'There's worse-looking lads in my year.'

The kissing went on. And on. Man, she really loves that donkey. Fairy magic must be powerful.

Rio stretched her legs out in front of her. 'So, have you ever done that?'

'What, kissed a farmyard animal? I don't think so.'

Rio laughed. 'No, you spoon. I mean, have you ever kissed someone?'

I suddenly went all hot, as if someone had cranked the radiator. 'You mean like a girl?'

'Or a boy,' she said, holding her hands up. 'I make no assumptions.'

I gulped. 'No. Have you?'

She shook her head. 'Can't say I have.'

It went quiet. The blinking lights of a plane coming into land glided through the black sky outside the window.

'They say your first kiss is rubbish,' said Rio. 'Well, Simone told me that, anyway.'

'Really?'

Rio nodded firmly. 'Best to just get it out of the way.'

Puck, the mischievous fairy came back on screen, giggling at the chaos he had unleashed. 'Is that right?' I said.

Rio shuffled closer to me. I hoped she couldn't hear my heart whacking against my chest. 'Yep,' she said. 'Just get it out of the way and get on with your life. No pressure.'

I nodded and concentrated really hard on the

screen. Why did Shakespeare have to use such weird words?

'You're not very good at taking hints are you, Ollie?' she said, shuffling even closer.

'What are you saying?' I asked.

She rolled her eyes so hard they almost did a loop-the-loop. 'I'm saying, shall we be each other's first kiss?'

I tried to reply, but I had no idea what to say and just ended up making a noise like a seal falling off a cliff.

'Look, it doesn't mean we're going to get married or anything. It's just . . . you never know what's going to happen, so we should probably, you know, seize the opportunity. If you want, that is.'

'Y-Yeah, I do,' I squeaked.

Rio turned in her seat and sat cross-legged like she always does in the chair by my bed. She smelled like gummy strawberries. Makes sense really, she'd eaten tons of them during the film. She reached up and held my face in her hands, then leaned in and kissed me on the lips. It only lasted about three seconds, but it made my entire body tingle. It was the exact opposite of the Puke Pit.

CHAPTER
18

I'm attempting Maths homework when there's a knock on my bedroom door. Mum gives me a second before walking in.

'Everything OK?' she asks, a little uneasily.

'Yeah, fine,' I say. 'How about you?'

'Can't complain.' Mum picks up a dirty T-shirt from the floor and drops it in my wash basket, before sitting on the edge of my bed.

'Jordan, I just wanted to apologize,' she says. 'I acted completely irrationally and I wanted you to know that I'm proud of you. Of both of you.'

Mum knew I'd started making the soup at school, but she hadn't talked about it before now.

I gulp and close my book. 'Um, thanks.'

Mum gives me a thin smile. 'So how did it go today?'

'Not too bad,' I say. 'The soup could have been better, though.'

She frowns. 'What do you mean?'

'They preferred your soups to mine.'

Mum chuckled. 'Of course they did. What recipe did you use?'

'Mr Grimshaw made it.'

Mum tuts and rolls her eyes theatrically. 'The old crusty that runs your school? No wonder they hated it. I'll be back in a sec.'

She gets up and goes downstairs, before returning a minute later with a tattered notebook.

'What's that?' I ask.

'My recipe book,' she replies. 'Every soup I've ever made is in here.' She holds it out to me and I go to take it, but she tightens her grip. 'Guard it with your life,' she says.

She lets me take the book and I flip through. Each page, in Mum's pristine handwriting, features a different recipe, along with detailed instructions on how to make it.

'Wow,' I say. 'Thanks, Mum.'

And it's now I realize it's more than just a book. For Mum to help out with something she was so against just yesterday must have taken a lot out of her.

'More than just soup,' I whisper to myself.

'What's that?' asks Mum, confused.

'Nothing,' I say.

CHAPTER
19

I have Mum's recipe book open on the worktop in the Food Tech kitchen. Today, I'm attempting chicken and sweetcorn and I'm determined to get going before Mr Grimshaw arrives and starts making hippy stew or whatever. I'm about to start chopping when the door opens. I spin around to see Maxwell, Imran, and Daria walk in.

'Oh. Hello.'

Maxwell smiles at me. 'We've come to help.'

They stand next to me at the counter. 'Seriously?' I ask.

'Mr Grimshaw was after volunteers and we thought, why not?' says Imran.

'Besides, this is the Soup Movement!' says Daria. 'Did you know you got a shout-out from Midlake Darston last night?'

Midlake Darston is a famous YouTuber. And

I do know. I was alerted to it when I ran into Abi's room last night thinking she was being attacked by some kind of mountain lion, only to find it was just her, hysterically pawing at her laptop screen.

'So come on,' says Maxwell, rolling up his sleeves. 'What do you need us to do?'

My suspicious brain can't help but wonder if this is some kind of trap, so I scan Maxwell's face for the tiniest sign that he's messing with me, a smirk, anything. But his expression is completely neutral.

'OK,' I say. 'You all need to wash your hands first. Then we'll get going.'

We get to work chopping and dicing. There are so many of us, we manage to get two batches made. We put one batch (leek and potato) in the fridge to warm up tomorrow.

I was right to trust them. They did everything according to the recipes, and were happy to help.

'Same time tomorrow?' says Maxwell. 'We'll try and get Will to come up, but don't hold your breath on that one.'

Yeah, I've got a feeling he'll be busy.

I put the four flasks in my bag and cycle over to the loading bay. This batch goes down a lot better than yesterday's. The magic of Mum's recipe book.

Abi's not here today because she's on a college trip, so there's no filming and everyone seems a bit more relaxed. Daniela sits on the edge of the deck and sketches us. It only takes her five minutes, but it looks amazing.

'This is really good today, Jordan,' says Harry. 'The others are going to be proper jealous if they find out.'

'Others?' I say. 'What others?'

Harry drained the last of the soup and wiped his mouth with the back of his hand. 'We're not the only homeless people in Pondstead, you know.'

'Just the best!' the Captain barks.

Harry chuckles. 'Something like that.'

'So where are the rest of them?' I ask.

'All over,' he says. 'But at the minute, a load of them are in the old church hall. There used to be a little shelter there, but they lost their funding and it got closed down.'

The Captain growls. 'Penny pinching slugs!'

'They managed to break in the other week and some of them are living in there illegally now,' says Harry, tapping the side of his nose.

My face goes all hot. How much must it cost to

keep a church hall open? It's just so unfair.

'Maybe we can help them, too,' I say.

'Sounds good,' says Harry. 'Shall we go over and take a look, get some numbers?'

'Is it far?' I ask.

'Kind of,' says Harry. 'We'll get there quicker if we take your bike.'

I look at the bike, then at Harry. 'How's that going to work?'

Harry chuckles. 'Hey, I can still pedal, mate.' He picks up my bike and hops on. 'Come on, I'll give you a backie.'

Oh God. I carefully get on and Harry waves goodbye to the others and moves us off. We coast down the street and through the park, past Harry's tent. He whoops as we pick up speed.

'I haven't been on a bike in years!' he says. 'To be honest, I wasn't sure I could still do it.'

The bike wobbles a little and I let out a shriek. If Mum could see me now, she'd probably ground me for the rest of my life. I'm not even wearing my stupid, comedy helmet.

I screw my eyes shut as he careers out of the park and onto the street, where he hops off the kerb and zooms us across the road.

'The old shelter is just at the end, here,' he yells over the wind whizzing past us. Most of the buildings on the street are industrial units with graffitied shutters, and the pavement is uneven. Harry picks up the pace a little, but then he screams an A-grade swear word and pumps the brakes. AAARGH! The bike bucks me off like an angry bull and I'm thrown up the wall before landing in a crumpled heap on the floor. Ouch. I sit up and survey the damage. I've scraped my hand a bit, but other than that, I'm not too bad.

I see the cause of the crash. A postman's trolley. He must have wheeled it around the corner just as we were approaching. The postman—a red-faced man about Dad's age—looks like he's going to have a heart attack.

'Oh, God, are you OK?' He approaches Harry, who's lying on the other side of the big, red trolley.

Harry groans and rubs his face. I get up to see if he's alright. The postman screams. What's wrong with him?

I run over and see his face is frozen in horror. 'Oh, no,' he squeaks. 'OH NO!'

I follow the direction of his finger until I see why he's so freaked out. I can't help but crack up.

'What are you laughing at?' he shrieks. 'He's sliced his leg off!'

This time, the laughter is uncontrollable. Sure enough, Harry's prosthetic has fallen off.

Harry sits up and picks up his leg and the postman has to lean on his trolley, probably to keep from fainting.

'Don't worry about it, mate,' he says. 'It'll grow back.'

I don't remember the last time I've laughed so much. At least it helped me forget about my skinned hand.

We reach the church hall, pushing the bike. It's a rundown building with a stone plaque next to the door, saying 'This stone was laid by the Rev. Archibald Cranleigh—8th August 1899.' Harry pushes the flaking door open and leads me inside.

We find about ten people in there. Some of them are lying on mattresses, others are crouched around a little table, playing cards.

A bloke with a long beard looks up from the beat-up paperback he's reading.

'Oh, hello, Harry. I was worried you were from the council. Who's this, your little brother?'

'Alright, Gus,' says Harry. 'Nah, this is Jordan.

He runs a charity.'

That sounded weird, but I kind of do, don't I? Who knew this was where that pinky swear would get me?

Gus gets up and gives me a smile. 'They get younger and younger. So what does your charity do, Jordan?'

It seems weird that he hasn't heard about it when it's become so well known, but then again I can't imagine he gets to go on the Internet that much.

'We make soup for hungry people,' I say.

'Plenty of those around here,' he says. 'Well, for now at least.'

'What do you mean?' Harry asks.

'Well, this is technically council property, even though they don't want to pay for it, so they could turn up at any moment and kick us out.'

'Why's that?' I ask. 'Do they need the building for something?'

'Nope,' he replies. 'They just wouldn't want us in it.'

This is like Safebuys all over again. What is it with taking things from poor people for no reason whatsoever? Wait until Abi hears about this.

'But that's stupid,' I say.

Gus chuckles. 'You don't have to tell me, mate. Nothing we can do, though.'

'Nothing?' I say.

Gus wearily shakes his head. I decide to change the subject to something I can help with.

'I'll have a batch of soup brought over to you tomorrow lunchtime. How many people are here?'

Gus does a quick head count. 'Ten, give or take.'

I do the maths in my head. It's going to take a lot of hard work, but at least I have a team now. Looks like the Soup Movement is growing.

To: Abi xx
From: Fernando Pacha

Hi guys,

Sorry if my English is bad. I am from Brasil.

I have started a Soup Movement in my home town of Santo André. Every day we make a big pot and within an hour it's all gone.

We have started our own YouTube channel (*Sopa de Justica*) to encourage others in Brasil to join us. Please consider giving us a shout-out.

Thank you,
Fernando

A GREAT BALDY

'I think it's time, don't you?' said Rio.

'Time for what?' I asked.

It was just Mum by the bed at the time. Dad was down in the office trying to sort out a parking ticket for the week. He's always doing stuff like that; buying TV cards, downloading apps for my tablet, going over my homework. It's as if he wants to be 'useful' all the time.

Rio made a noise like a razor and ran a hand across her scalp.

'Oh, I think he's OK, dear,' said Mum, sounding startled.

Rio scrunched up her nose. 'Is he? He's starting to look like a monk.'

I touched the growing bald patch at the back of my head. 'Maybe she's got a point, Mum.'

'But what if you get a cold?' said Mum.

Rio spluttered with laughter, then tried to make it seem like she was coughing. God, Mum, I've got cancer and I never go outside. Who cares about a cold?

'I'll wear a hat,' I said.

So about an hour later, we went to the bathroom and Pravina the nurse shaved my head. I watched in the mirror as my hair fell to the floor like leaves off a tree.

I stared at my reflection under the harsh light right above my head. I looked like a different person.

'See?' said Rio to my mum. 'He's got a lovely shaped head. He's going to make a great baldy.'

Mum looked at her for a second, then burst into tears.

CHAPTER
20

How am I supposed to run a Soup Movement when I have to do PE? By the time I'm showered and dressed, I'm running ten minutes late. Luckily, my team has started without me, warming up yesterday's batch.

When I told Mr Grimshaw about our expansion yesterday, he winked at me and said, 'I'll hook you up, dude.' This morning, I came to school to find he had brought in a wooden trailer to attach to the back of my bike, along with ten extra flasks.

'Consider it a donation,' he says.

I leave the others to prepare tomorrow's batch while I take today's downstairs and load it onto my new trailer. I line them up carefully so they won't fall over the side as I pedal. I now have two stops to make: the loading bay and the church hall. Then I might get a chance to have a quick lunch myself.

I head down the school drive, ignoring the yells of 'Helmet's got a trailer'. It's funny how my new 'fame' hasn't really changed things at school. I thought it might make me more popular, but if anything, it's made everyone think I'm stuck up, like I'm too good for them. I don't understand humans.

I'm turning the corner outside school when I have to squeeze the brakes to avoid a figure standing in front of me. It's not the postman this time.

'Fancy running into you here,' says Will.

'I literally nearly ran into you,' I say, trying to get my breath back.

He steps closer to me and puts his hand on my handlebars. His mouth is a tense line and his eyes are narrowed.

'When are you going home, Helmet?'

I shrug. 'Quarter past three, same time as always.'

'No, I mean when are you going back to the city? There's loads of tramps there. You'd be set for life.'

I ease the bike backwards until it's free of his grip. 'I'm not going back, Will. Like it or not, I'm here to stay.'

He kicks my tyre, sending shudders through the bike and making the flasks tremble in the back.

'You don't get to call me Will,' he grumbles. 'You address me as William, got it? Only my mates call me Will. Not that I see them anymore.'

'You're crazy,' I say. 'For one thing, you're completely welcome to come up with them any time you want.'

'Yeah, well, I don't want,' he says. 'Because the only reason you're doing this is to get rid of me.'

'What?'

'You know what I mean. I had a bit of fun with that tent bloke so you decided to make me look like a terrible person by becoming the patron saint of tramps,' he yells.

I shake my head. 'Are you so arrogant that you think everything is about you?'

Will points at me, his hand trembling. 'You're going to wish you never came here.'

I push off and cycle away as quick as the trailer will allow. Will is the craziest person I've ever met, and I say that as someone who lives with my mum.

I drop the first batch off at the loading bay, then head over to the church hall. Abi is already outside against the wall, filming.

ABI: Hey guys, this is Abi xx at a new location, where the homeless of Pondstead are forced to congregate. I've been asked by them not to give away the whereabouts of this place, because they are here illegally.

I go inside and start handing out the flasks. Gus comes along and introduces me to everyone. It's all a bit of a blur so I struggle to take it all in, but I do my best to remember everyone's names. What amazes me is how different everyone is. I think when you see homeless people on the streets, you lump them all together, and don't realize that they've all got their own stories and their own lives.

I'm glad they all seem to appreciate the soup, anyway. Maxwell, Imran, and Daria are doing a great job. I just wish Will wasn't hanging over the whole thing.

CHAPTER
21

Dad has been quiet since he got in from work. I know he's tired a lot, but today it's different. He looks tense. His shoulders are hunched as he pokes at his dinner with his fork, stabbing at the chunks of chicken like he's got a grudge against them.

'Everything OK, love?' Mum asks.

'Fine,' he replies, not looking up from his dinner.

It goes quiet again. All I can hear is the cat clock on the wall, its eyes and tail wagging from side to side as time passes.

'You know, Dad, it's important not to bottle things up,' says Abi. 'Stress is the leading killer of men your age.'

Dad sighs and smiles bitterly. 'Thank you, Abi. That's exactly what I wanted to hear.'

'Just saying,' says Abi, holding her hands up.

'Alright,' Dad throws his knife and fork down

with a clatter. 'I didn't want to burden you lot with it, but it was going to come out sooner or later, so here we are. Kellmans is struggling. The MD called a meeting today and said there's going to have to be redundancies.'

Mum reaches over and touches Dad's arm. 'Try not to worry. They won't want to lose you.'

Dad shifts in his chair. 'The world's changing, Claire. Young people don't read magazines any more. They get all their information from the Internet and these . . .' He gestures at Abi while he searches for the word. 'Influencers.'

It's only now I notice how crumpled he looks, both his clothes and his face. 'I've been working there twenty years now.' He stops and shakes his head like it's the first time he's realized that fact. 'Twenty years.'

Silence descends once again. 'I'm sure it'll be fine,' says Mum.

'I hope so,' says Dad, raising an eyebrow at me. 'Otherwise we'll be the ones needing soup.'

After dinner, Abi calls me into her room. I feel privileged. She never does that. I once went in there to borrow her phone charger and she jumped out from behind her wardrobe and gave me a dead arm.

'I went down to the loading bay today and spoke to Harry,' she says.

'What, he allowed you an interview?'

Abi nods. 'I'm as surprised as you are.' She clicks the video on her laptop. 'Have a look.'

ABI: Hey guys, It's Abi xx. I'm here today with the man who helped kick-start the Soup Movement, Harry.

HARRY: Oh, I don't know about that. I just introduced Jordan to some friends, that's all.

ABI: OK, so Harry, I'm going to ask you the same question I ask everyone; what's your story?

HARRY: Just had some bad luck . . . made bad decisions. The usual, know what I mean?

ABI: Sure, but you're a veteran, aren't you?

HARRY: Suppose so. Couple of tours in Iraq.

ABI: And, sorry if this is too personal, but you were injured on duty?

HARRY: That's right. You want to take a look?

The camera pans down and we see his prosthetic leg.

HARRY: IED did that. If the medics weren't so close, I'd have probably died.

ABI: And what happened after that?

HARRY: Months in hospital. So many operations, I lost count. Months of physio, learning how to walk on the prosthetic. Then it was, 'Off you go. Good luck.'

ABI: And how did you cope?

HARRY: Not well. Not . . . not well. I got sad. I don't know if you'd call it depressed, but I wasn't happy. And I'd have nightmares, too. I'd dream about being back in Iraq. I'd dream about getting out of bed and finding my bedroom floor covered with IEDs.

ABI: That sounds terrible. Did you have family to help you through it?

HARRY (shifts uncomfortably): I had my dad. Mum died when I was a teenager. My sister lives overseas so she wasn't really around. Dad did his best but . . . I wasn't in a good place, you know what I mean? I was angry all the while. Angry with the world. I said things to him I didn't mean. I . . . I did bad stuff. I've . . . I've got to go.

After the video ends, Abi looks at me, eyebrows raised.

'Wow,' I whisper.

'I think that took a lot out of him,' says Abi.

I can understand it. I mean, I've never told anyone at school about having cancer. The idea of talking about it is scary. And besides, I don't want them to see me differently. To pity me.

'Hey,' I say to Abi, changing the subject to stop myself falling down a rabbit hole I don't want to go down. 'What do you think about what Dad was saying?'

Abi shrugs. 'You know as well as I do he's hated that job for years. Maybe doing something else wouldn't be such a bad thing for him. Whatever happens, I hope he doesn't end up working from home like Mum. I'm off to uni soon, so it doesn't matter to me, but you really don't want two of them hanging around the place.'

I push my luck and sit on the edge of Abi's bed. 'When did things get so complicated?' I ask. 'Was it when I got sick? Did I start it?'

Abi spins around on the chair and looks at me blankly. 'Jordan, mate,' she says. 'You're alright and everything, but you're not the centre of the universe.'

My face flushes. 'What do you mean?'

'Life was never easy, Jordan,' she says. 'There have always been problems and twists and kinks, way before you got sick. What probably happened is *that* was when you started to notice.'

I tut. I hate to admit it, but she's got a point. The world really has gone crazy.

CHAPTER
22

Maxwell, Imran, and Daria are looking extra sharp today. Not that they ever show up looking shabby, but today, they've put in the extra effort. Abi is coming in at lunchtime to film them preparing the next batch. It's going to be for a video about the expansion of the Pondstead Soup Movement.

'Do you think your sis will be cool with me plugging my gaming channel?' Imran asks.

I laugh. 'Probably not.'

Imran tuts and yanks up his shirt to reveal an IMRANZ TEKKERZ vest. 'So I had this made for nothing?'

I turn the corner on my way to registration and see Will, leaning against his locker. I get that uneasy, seasick feeling that comes when I see someone I dreamt about the night before. I can't remember exactly what happened, just him chasing me through the children's ward with a sword of some kind. You know, standard stuff.

At least he's not looking at me now. He's staring straight ahead, while in front of him, Mr Grimshaw is launching into a lecture.

'You need to have respect for others, my man,' he says. 'Especially when they're helping the community.'

Will shrugs. 'I was just checking the soup was alright. Don't want them getting poisoned.'

I step around the corner and listen. What was he doing?

'I don't buy that for a second, man. I caught you about to tip it down the sink.'

I clench my fists. It's one thing to mess with me, but that soup is for homeless people. What's his problem?

'I know things aren't easy for you, Will, but this kind of thing needs to stop,' Grimshaw goes on. 'Let's face it, it's not the first time I've had to speak to you about your behaviour, is it?'

Will doesn't answer.

'Well, I'll be making sure the kitchen door is locked at all times from now on, and if we have to have any more talks like this, you're going to be looking at exclusion. You dig?'

Now that would be nice. Let's hope that happens sooner rather than later.

We've got the soup production line down to an art. Daria starts warming yesterday's batch, while Maxwell and Imran get to work making today's. Then, I pour the warmed-up stuff into flasks, while Daria joins Maxwell and Imran, chopping and stirring. We have music playing and it's actually a good laugh.

Then, I take the flasks, first to the loading bay, then to the church hall, and return the empty ones to school to be washed.

Today, Abi shows up wearing a visitor's lanyard and tells the three of them to act naturally while she films. She gets plenty of close-ups of the soup prep, as well as little interviews with the crew. I can tell she switches the camera off when Imran starts talking about his gaming channel. Just as I predicted.

I head out on my bike to the loading bay. When I give Harry his flask, he says sorry for walking out of Abi's interview.

'That's alright,' I say. 'You don't have to talk about anything you don't want to.'

He shrugs. 'In a way, it felt better to talk. To begin with, anyway.'

Oh, I don't know, my stupid brain says. *We've always found it's better to keep things in. Let them fester up here. That's our time-honoured method.*

'I didn't know about your dad,' I say.

Harry takes a sip of soup. 'No reason why you should. I wasn't going to mention him to your sis, but.' He sniffs. 'It just came out.'

'Don't you want to get in touch with him?'

'Well he's moved, so I don't know where he is,' says Harry. 'He wouldn't want to hear from me anyway. He told me that.'

I go to leave it, to get back on my bike and go over to the church hall, but a voice in my head stops me. It's not my usual, stupid, brain, it's the opposite. It's light rather than darkness. I know exactly who it is. *Go back,* it says. *You know what to do.*

'What's your dad's name?' I ask.

'Colin,' he replies.

I nod, taking a mental note, that voice still chattering in my head, urging me on.

'And where are you from originally?'

'Belford,' says Harry. 'I don't know if Dad still lives there, though.'

I take the remaining flasks up to the church hall and find that the old ones have been washed up for me.

'Well, we've still got running hot water,' says Gus. 'For now, anyway.'

When I leave the church hall and start heading back to school, I see a shadow disappear around the corner ahead, where Harry and I had that accident with the postman. It moves fast, almost like it's gliding. For a horrible second, I think it's one of the dark figures from my nightmares come to find me in the real world, but I shake my head and carry on pedalling. It was probably just someone out for a jog.

Man, maybe all this hard work is making me go crazy.

THE HOSPITAL BLOG

GOING HOME

Dr Kanelos came around this morning. I'm going home in two days. I don't know what to think. I mean, I'm happy, but at the same time . . .

I'll be back in a month for the next round of chemo, anyway. Going back to normal will be weird, though. Whatever 'normal' is. I've just found out that Mum and Dad have put the house up for sale and are on about moving us out of the city. Mum's got it into her head that pollution from cars might have made me ill. But everywhere has cars. Unless they're planning on moving us to the eighteenth century.

After everyone had left, I went and sat in the chair by Rio's bed. She swiped her tablet off and smiled at me.

'Afternoon, bald buddy.'

I rubbed my head. I'm just about getting used to it, but when I get out of hospital and everyone sees me,

I'm going to have to get used to it all over again.

I tapped the arms of the chair. I knew what I had to say, but I didn't know how to say it.

'Don't worry about it, I know,' said Rio.

'Huh?'

She sat up a little, fluffing up her pillow behind her back. 'It's only a poxy, blue curtain separating us, mate. Not exactly soundproofed.'

Makes sense. When the doctor draws it around your bed, you feel like you're in your own room. 'And, are you OK about that?'

'Yeah, I'm dead happy for you, Ollie,' she said. 'I'm pleased actually, cos I've got news for you, too.'

I raised my eyebrows.

'You're not the only one going home.'

'Seriously?'

Rio nodded excitedly. 'Yeah, I found out today! What are the odds?'

'Wow, that's brilliant,' I said. 'Have they said when you've got to come back?'

'Nope. Indefinite leave. Freed from prison.' She smiled, her eyes twinkling. 'I'm going to miss you, Ollie.'

I gulped down the brick in my throat. 'We'll keep in touch though, right?'

'Too right we will,' said Rio. 'You're not getting rid of me that easy. And besides, we have to meet up a year after we pinky swore to see how the mitzvah thing is getting on.'

'Right,' I said. 'The pinky swear is sacred.'

Rio thumped my arm. 'Course it is.'

CHAPTER
23

I don't know why I thought Harry's dad was going to be on Facebook. I mean, he's probably really old. I know Facebook is for old people, but not *that* old.

Next I google 'Colin Longley Belford', but the few it comes up with aren't the right age to be Harry's dad. This is going to be harder than I thought.

I lean back in my chair and rub my eyes. I love doing the Soup Movement but a solid school week of it is tiring. I'm about to rethink my 'find Harry's dad' strategy, when my door flies open.

'Ever heard of knocking, Abi?' I say. 'I could have been naked in here!'

Abi ignores me. Her face is flushed red and she has that vertical line between her eyes that she gets when she's really ticked off.

'Have you heard?'

'About what?'

'Someone has tipped the council off about the church hall and they've given them notice to leave within the next seven days.'

I feel like I've been slapped. 'Who would do that? They weren't causing any trouble!'

'They're going nowhere,' says Abi. 'We've taken Safebuys on and won, what are Pondstead Council going to do?'

'OK,' I say, hoping to God it doesn't mean having to lie on the floor again. 'So what's the first step?'

'We get down there and tell the world,' she says. 'Come on.'

She turns and stomps out before I can ask if it's OK if I change out of my pyjamas first.

When we arrive at the church hall, there's a definite tension in the air. Everyone looks sad and worried. More than they normally do.

Gus greets us by the door. 'Well,' he says. 'I knew this day would come eventually, I just didn't think it would be so soon.'

'Someone tipped them off,' a bloke built like a heavyweight boxer growls, glaring at us under the thick ridge of his brow.

Abi's jaw drops. 'It wasn't us!'

The boxer man crosses his tree trunk arms. 'Well, I don't know what to think. Before you showed up, no one knew we were here. Now, all of a sudden we're in this mess.'

'Calm down, Marlon,' says Gus. 'Getting angry won't change anything.'

'You can't think this was us, can you, Gus?' I ask him.

Gus doesn't answer straight away. His face twists into a grimace. 'No,' he says. 'I don't think so, anyway.'

'We'll fight this all the way,' says Abi. 'We won't let them win.'

This Marlon bloke stands up slowly, his knees cracking like gunfire. 'That's what I thought you'd say,' he says. 'It's almost as if you've shopped us to the council to create some publicity for your stupid YouTube channel.'

'That is ridiculous,' says Abi, more aggressively than I would ever dare. 'He's being ridiculous, isn't he, guys?'

Abi looks around at the others, but no one will make eye contact with her. Oh, God, do they really think we're behind this? Surely there has to be some way we can prove it wasn't us?

Gus places a hand on both of our shoulders. 'I think it would be best if you guys leave,' he says. 'Emotions are running high, you know how it is.'

When we get outside, Abi aims a kick at a bin. Luckily for her, she misses. 'Who could have done this?' she asks, but I don't answer because I'm too busy thinking. I remember when I came out the other day and saw that shadow flitting around the corner. It was as if they were watching the hall but didn't want to be seen.

My instinct is to reject it, but the more I think about it, the more sense it seems to make.

CHAPTER
24

I couldn't think of anything else over the weekend. There were times when I wrote it off. After all, it could have been anyone that reported them to the council. It could have just been a passer-by, or maybe that scary Marlon bloke upset the wrong person and they took revenge in the only way that wouldn't get them beaten to within an inch of their lives. I don't know.

I try to take my mind off things by resuming my search for Harry's dad. Searching for him by name was a bust, so I'd have to try and find another friend or family member and get to him that way. Surely Harry himself had to have some kind of social media presence, right? Wrong! Either he'd never been on them, or he'd deleted all his accounts. Either way, it was another dead end. But a search for his name and 'Belford' does turn up something. It's a really old news article from the *Belford Observer*.

LOCAL LADS SHIP OUT TO IRAQ
By Stephen Jones
3rd March 2003

As troops begin to move out to the conflict in the Middle East, a few Belford Boys are among their number. Harry Longley, 21, and Barry 'Beefy' Drake, 23, are both set to ship out with the Mercian Regiment next week.

'People tell me I'm brave, but I don't really see it,' says cheeky chappy Harry, who attended Yarrow High school. 'I'm just there to do a job for my country.'

Hmm. Now this could be a way in. If I find this Beefy bloke, he might be able to point me in the right direction. I put his name into every social-media app I can think of, but there's no trace of him. I slam the laptop shut and flop down on my bed. I thought everyone in the world was on at least one of those things, and I've somehow managed to find three that are on none of them.

CHAPTER
25

I'm in a toilet cubicle at school. I don't normally like
to use them, but when you've got to go, you've got to
go. I'm nearly finished when I hear heavy footsteps
followed by the door next to me slamming shut.

'You in there, Helmet?'

'What do you want, Will?' I say, recognizing his
voice straight away.

'I hope you're going to wash your hands,' he says.
'I'd hate to have you closed down for bad hygiene.'

Up till now, I'd planned on calmly trying to get a
confession out of him, but the anger and frustration
can't help but come spilling out.

'You did it, didn't you?' I say, leaning as close to
the divider as I dared. 'You told the council about
the church hall.'

Will laughs. 'I just don't like to see the law being
broken, that's all.'

I grip the toilet-roll dispenser. 'You're sick.'

'And you're a loser, Helmet,' he shoots back. 'You always will be. As soon as this stupid soup thing goes belly-up, you'll never see the others again. They're only using you to get Internet famous, anyway.'

'Shut up,' I whisper, trying to ignore my stupid brain telling me he's right about everything.

'Want to hop over here and make me?' he says.

'The people in the church hall think me and my sister told the council,' I say.

Will laughs, an explosion bursting from his mouth. I spring out of my cubicle and try to open his. I don't know what I'd do if I got through, but he's locked it anyway.

'That's amazing,' he chuckles. 'I didn't realize I'd be causing this much chaos. Not only is your stupid Soup Movement dying, but now a building full of tramps hate your guts! Yes!'

I kick the door, then yelp in pain. It's harder than I was expecting.

At lunch, I hobble up to the kitchen. Maxwell, Daria, and Imran are already there putting their aprons on.

'Here he is!' says Maxwell. 'How's it going, boss?'

I mumble something and look at the floor. What Will said has cut through, even if I didn't want it to.

'When's Abi uploading that video of us?' Daria asks.

'Yeah, I was refreshing the feed all night last night,' says Imran.

See? my stupid brain says. *They're nothing more than fame hungry posers. I wouldn't trust them as far as I could kick them.*

'Don't know,' I say.

It goes quiet and I can tell they're looking at each other like 'what's his problem?' My phone rings. Abi. What's going on? I don't think she's ever called me. She always texts.

'Hello? What's happening? Is someone dead?'

'What?' she says. 'No. Well, not yet. The reason I'm calling is I've been worrying about you going to the church hall on your own. I thought maybe you should stay away for a while.'

I'd been thinking about it, too. Of course I don't want to go in there. That Marlon bloke is terrifying. But I can't abandon them just because they're suspicious of me. That's not what the pinky swear is about.

'I won't go in there,' I say. 'Promise.'

After dropping the first batch at the loading bay, I bike over to the church hall. I'm finding I'm getting used to it now. I'm not completely out of breath when I get there and my legs don't feel like they're going to drop off anymore.

I linger at the corner where me and Harry crashed into the postman and make sure no one is outside, then I coast over, and place the flasks outside the front door before making a quick exit. I know they might not want to see me right now, but they have to know we're still looking out for them. It's more than just soup.

SHE'S OUT

I don't know why I'm still writing these, I'm not even in hospital anymore. I guess I'm just bored. Truth be told, I'm really missing Rio. It's weird waking up, looking to my left and seeing my Hulk poster rather than Rio sitting up in bed making a playlist with her tongue clamped between her teeth in concentration. I miss walking down the corridor to the rec room and watching TV with her. Even the worst film in the world can be made better with her commentary.

Ross's mum made him come over to visit, but like his hospital visit, we didn't talk much. So I was kind of relieved when my phone buzzed.

I'M OUT, OLLIE! I TUNNELLED MY WAY OUT OF SHAWSHANK. Here's a lil snapshot of where I am. Xx

She attached a photo of a view along Brighton pier.

Wow, her family don't mess around. Still, knowing Rio, she probably insisted on being taken straight there. She loves Brighton.

'What are you smiling at?' Ross asked.

'Rio,' I replied.

'That weird girl from hospital?' he said.

'Yeah,' I said, still smiling hugely. 'That weird girl.'

CHAPTER
26

I'm doing some searching around the Pondstead
Council website and apparently, there's no way to
find out who has reported someone. I thought there
might have been some kind of official paperwork
I could have got, to show them that it wasn't me or
Abi.

There's a hesitant little knock at my door and
Dad walks in with a mug of tea. He's been kind of
mopey the past few days, going to bed early and not
talking very much. It's weird without his constant
stream of dodgy Dad jokes.

'What's this?' he says, nodding at my laptop
screen. 'Homework?'

'It's more soup related,' I say, which I realize is a
sentence that would have sounded insane a month or
two ago.

Dad sits on the edge of my bed and takes a sip of

his tea. 'Oh yeah?'

I tell him about the shelter being closed down but leave off the stuff about Will, because if I get into all that, he'll probably end up storming down to the school and I just don't have the energy for it.

Dad lets out a long breath so he sounds like a dinghy with a hole in it. 'The older I get, the less I understand this world.'

I gulp. That's not exactly the most reassuring thing I've ever heard. I remember, as a little kid, I thought adults all knew exactly what to do in all situations. I thought when I turned eighteen, or maybe twenty-one, everything would click into place and stuff would finally make sense. But when Dad says stuff like this, or when Mum freaked out about the Soup Movement, it makes me realize that maybe I'm always going to be winging it.

'So what's going to happen?' says Dad. 'The council turfs them out onto the street and the building is allowed to go derelict?'

'Pretty much,' I say. 'If I had the money, I'd buy it myself and let them stay.'

Dad reaches over and ruffles my hair. 'You're a good lad, Jordan.'

Before he can leave, I tell him about my other

'homework': finding Harry's dad. He scooches up closer to me.

'Bit of detective work, eh?' he says. 'So what do you have so far?'

'Not much,' I say. 'There's no trace of Harry or his dad on social media, so I decided to look into his army buddies. I found one, but he's not on there, either.'

Dad frowns and purses his lips, the way he always does when he's trying to figure something out. 'What's his name?'

'Barry Drake,' I reply. 'His nickname's Beefy.'

Dad grabs the laptop, pulls his glasses out of his top pocket and starts typing. It's only about half a minute later when he says, 'Ah. Here we are.' Then his face falls. 'Oh.'

I take the laptop back and read another piece from the *Belford Observer*.

DARKEST DAY FOR TOWN AS LOCAL MAN KILLED IN IRAQ AND ANOTHER SEVERELY INJURED

By Stephen Jones
8th June 2006

Belford is in mourning after local soldier Barry 'Beefy' Drake was killed in an IED attack on the outskirts of Baghdad during a routine patrol.

The popular 26-year-old was on his third tour in the region when the tragedy struck. His sister Hannah, 32, described Barry as having a 'heart of gold.'

Also caught up in the attack was 24-year-old Harry Longley, who is currently at a military hospital in Germany receiving treatment for what have been described as 'life-changing injuries'.

'He's never talked about that,' I say, my voice caught in my throat.

'Can't be easy,' says Dad. 'He's probably got survivor's guilt.'

A cold shiver runs down my spine, and Dad must notice, because he squeezes my shoulder and gives me a warm smile.

'Still,' Dad goes on. 'Looks like we've hit a dead end. Tell you what, leave it with me. We've got ways of tracking people down at the magazine. If I manage, I'll let you know.'

'Wow,' I say, 'thanks, Dad.'

Dad shrugs. 'I might as well do something useful at work, eh?

I'm on my way into school, now. I've got a plan. It
came to me last night in bed, just as I was about to
drop off. I sat upright, my heart pounding. Anyone
watching would have thought I was having one of
my nightmares.

Now, I still don't know if it's going to work,
but it's worth a go. This situation with the church
hall can't go on like this. Harry told me that they
wouldn't even let him in when he went for a shower,
because they thought he was in league with me and
Abi.

At lunchtime, I take a detour on my way to the
kitchen. Will is sitting alone on the wall outside
school. It's his regular hangout since he decided
to separate himself from the others. He sees me
coming and smirks.

'Alright, Helmet?' he says. 'I owe you a thank
you.'

'Really?' I say, flatly.

He juts out his jaw and nods. 'What you said
about the tramps hating you is the best laugh I've
had in years.'

'How did you know they weren't supposed to be
in there?' I ask.

Will goes cross-eyed and slaps himself on the forehead. 'DUH! Did you not see the sign on the door saying the property has been vacated?'

I tut. If someone had thought to take that down, he'd never have known.

'Yeah?' I say. 'And what did you say to them?'

'I sent them an email from a new account,' he says. 'Ooh, I'm a concerned resident and I don't think these homeless should be in that old church hall. I mean, what if one of them hurts themselves? Health and safety and all that.'

'What if all those people end up on the streets because of you?'

He shrugs. 'They'll just have to find somewhere else. Maybe somewhere that doesn't involve you walking around like you're Jesus.'

'What are you on about?'

'You heard,' he says, laughing breathily. 'You're doing this so people will like you. Let's face it, they thought you were boring before. You don't care about those people; it's all for attention. Well guess what? You got my attention.'

I reach inside my pocket and stop my phone recording. I've got what I need now.

'I'm not doing it for attention,' I say. 'I hate

attention.'

'Could have fooled me,' Will scoffs. 'Strutting around on the Internet like you're Midlake Darston.'

I try to step around him but he's in my face. 'The vlog was my sister's idea,' I say. 'The only reason I'm in favour is because it might encourage other people to do the same.'

'Yeah, right,' says Will, jabbing me in the chest. 'You're as selfish as anyone. Admit it.'

I grab his hand and wrench it away. 'You want to know the real reason I'm doing this?' I say.

Will folds his arms, a sarcastic smile plastered across his face. 'Go on, then.'

'I'm doing this because nearly a year ago, I made a promise to someone. Someone I cared about. We were both in hospital because we had cancer.'

Will's smile collapses. 'Shut up.'

'I've never told anyone else about that here,' I say. 'I wish the first person I'd told had been a close friend, but if it's the only way I can get you to leave me alone.'

'You did not have cancer,' he says. 'You're sick to lie about something like that.'

'Believe me or don't,' I say, 'but I'm in remission

now, and hopefully I'll stay that way. Not everyone is so lucky.'

'Prove it,' he says in a voice that sounds strangled.

I get my phone out and go to my photos. I can understand needing proof. I wouldn't want to think I'd been bullying a cancer survivor either. It doesn't take me long to find the photo I need. It's me and Rio sitting together in the rec room, both bald as babies. We'd just watched a horror film and she was laughing at me because I had to keep hiding my face at the scary bits. I allow myself to look at it for a few seconds, to really take it in. At one time, looking at this photo for any more than a couple of seconds was like putting my hand on a hot stove. But now I'm able to stand it a little longer. I show Will.

He narrows his eyes, studying it. He looks at me, then back at the photo, repeating the action again and again. Finally, he turns away. 'Alright, you can go,' he says, quietly.

'So, do you get it now?' I ask.

'I said you can go,' he says, his voice full of menace.

As I walk away, my head goes swimmy and I have to slow down.

The next half an hour is a blur. I go up to the kitchen and pick up the latest batch. I load it up, deliver it to the loading bay, and then the church hall, where this time, I walk inside.

Marlon sees me and gets up to stop me. 'What are you doing here?'

The sight of this enormous man looming in front of me finally snaps me out of my brain fug. 'I've brought your soup,' I squeak.

'Well, we don't want it, do we?' he says, gesturing around the room.

Some people shake their heads, others just stare at me.

'I've got something you need to hear,' I say, pulling out my phone.

'Not interested,' says Marlon. 'Go on, get out.'

Gus comes out of the kitchen at the back of the room, and I don't think I've ever been as glad to see anyone in my life. He seems to be the only person that can talk Marlon around.

'What is it, Jordan?' he says, standing between us.

I press play on the phone and turn it up so they can hear Will admit to sending the email to the council. Marlon's face grows grimmer as it goes on, and he cracks his knuckles.

'Well,' says Gus when it's over. 'I guess we owe you an apology.'

Marlon nods. 'Sorry, man.'

'It's fine,' I say. 'I can understand why you'd think it was us. The question is, what do we do now?'

'They're coming on Friday to throw us out,' says Gus. 'If we don't go quietly, they'll call the police to remove us. The way I see it, the only way to stop it is to cause enough of a stink that ordinary people stand with us and oppose it.'

I think about it, a plan formulating in my brain, encouraged by that voice, the voice that echoes back to the hospital, to the rec room, to the first time we locked our fingers together and vowed to make the world a better place.

ABI xx: DOWN AND OUT IN PONDSTEAD

ME: Um, hello everyone. I know you normally see Abi on here, but this time, you've got me. Sorry about that.

The reason is, I've had an idea and Abi reckoned I should be the one to tell you about it. Basically, I need a favour from you. The Pondstead Church Hall has been a vital shelter for the homeless community around here: somewhere for people to turn when they're desperate. A few months ago, Pondstead council withdrew their funding for it and decided that they wanted the property back, leaving them with nowhere to turn.

They did what they had to do. They gained access to the building and lived there illegally. The council has been tipped off about this, and now they're going to be forcibly removed this Friday.

Their only hope is if we stand up and be counted. So this Friday, we are going to form a human barrier around the hall. The more people show up, the stronger we will be. The address is in the description below. Please share this as widely as you can, because we are going to need every last one of you. We'll see you there.

This took sixteen attempts.

BEING CREATIVE

I'm back. In a weird way, I've been looking forward to it. Being at home was less fun than I thought it would be. For one thing, they have now officially sold the house and have very nearly bought another in a place called Pondstead. Abi and I tried to stage an intervention, but they wouldn't hear it. We're going and that's that.

To make things worse, for the whole month, Mum wouldn't let me do anything. And I mean anything. I couldn't even go to the shops on my own. All I was allowed to do was sit there, watch TV and get more jealous by the second as Rio sent me photos of all the cool stuff she was doing. As well as Brighton, she'd been to gigs with Simone up in Manchester, she'd been swimming, she'd even managed a weekend in France! She'd always send me little photos: bands on stage, the Eiffel Tower lit up against the evening sky. I wished my parents were a bit more relaxed like Rio's.

I tried to organize a meet-up one week when she would be home. I just really wanted to see her. I thought if I could get Mum to take me somewhere, she'd be cool with it. Well, Rio seemed dead keen, but then a few hours later, told me that she was being taken on another holiday, this time to Spain. Apparently, her nan has a villa out there.

So this is just a long way of saying that being in hospital won't be that different to being at home. Except for all the horrible chemo, of course.

When me and mum arrived at the ward, Kate was there to greet us. She gave us both a hug and asked Mum if she wanted a cup of tea. She remembered exactly how she likes it.

'Your old bed is free, if you're interested, Jordan?' she said.

I agreed. Why mess with a winning formula?

She led us down the corridor and into our little section. The smells and noises and weird wall paintings were all so familiar this time around, a bit like going back to your old primary school. The bed next door to me was curtained off as I arrived and I was left to settle in for a while before Dr Kanelos made his rounds.

I put my trusty old Star Wars T-shirt on with a pair of shorts. I've become a bit superstitious about that thing. I wore it on my first day first time round and now I feel like I've got to do the same again. I would say it's lucky, but it's clearly not. While I got changed, Mum went off to the rec room. I insisted. There's no way I want her hanging around round watching me get changed. She's all 'I used to wipe your bum when you were a baby' and I'm like, 'well, times change.'

I climbed into bed and pulled out my iPad. I could hear muffled voices from behind the curtain of next door's bed. I'm not that nosy really, but my ears automatically strained to make out what they were saying. They were talking quietly, but they sounded familiar. After a couple of minutes, the curtain was pulled back and Pravina came out, wheeling away some kind of machine with a cheery, 'See you in a bit, sweetpea.'

I glanced over at the bed through the corner of my eye. I'm going to be here for a while, so I should probably get used to whoever I'm sharing my half of the room with. When I saw her, I almost fell out of bed.

'Rio?'

'Oh, hello, Jordan,' said Rio's mum, quieter than I'd

ever heard her. 'I didn't know you were back. Rio's a bit tired at the moment.' She nodded at the bed where Rio lay with her eyes closed. She looked different. She'd lost weight. Her collarbone jutted out above her pyjama top.

'How long has she been back?' I asked.

Rio's mum frowned. 'From where?'

'From home.'

She gently massaged her forehead with her right hand. 'I don't know what you mean, sweetheart.'

Before I could ask anything else, Mum came back and said a quick hello to Rio's mum before blabbing on about how I need to start drinking kale smoothies or something like that. I wasn't listening, though. I picked up my phone and scrolled through mine and Rio's chat log. Past photo after photo. Beaches, meadows, famous Parisian landmarks. Not a single one of her. I googled 'Brighton pier' and looked at the image results. The fifth one along was identical to the one she'd sent.

Later, when her mum had stepped out and my mum was off for lunch, I went over to her bed.

'Rio?'

Besides the gentle rise and fall of her chest beneath the sheet, she was completely still.

'Rio, I can tell you're not really asleep.'

She opened an eye and I saw the pupil seek me out. 'Yes I am,' she said.

I sat in the chair. 'Why did you lie?'

She closed her eye again. I watched as her throat bobbed in a dry swallow. 'You call it lying, I call it being creative.'

'I'm serious, Rio.'

She slowly turned over and the curve of her spine sticking out made me gasp. 'Too tired right now,' she said. 'Talk later.'

I could see I wasn't going to get anything else out of her, so I went back to bed. As long as I live, I'll never understand her.

CHAPTER
27

Have you ever had the urge to sing? Like, you're feeling so good, so hopeful, that it bursts out of you? That's how I'm feeling right now.

We've been getting nonstop notifications from people saying they're coming to be part of the blockade. People from really far away, in some cases. School's been great, too. I didn't see Will all day, which I wouldn't have minded because I could have rubbed his nose in it, but still, I don't mind not having to deal with his nonsense.

So that's why I want to sing. I'm halfway down the garden path when I burst into song, something from my favourite playlist—this old one called 'I Fought the Law'. I'm not bothered about being heard. Mum's had to go to the office today, so there's no one around, anyway.

I take my bike around the back, chain it up,

unlock the door and go inside, all before I get to the first chorus.

'I fought the law,' I sing.

'And the law won!' comes the reply.

I freeze in my tracks, submerged in an icy chill. This house really is haunted. By singing ghosts. It's only when Dad appears in the doorway that I calm down slightly. Then burn with embarrassment.

'The Clash,' says Dad, shaking his head and staring into the distance as if recalling some precious memory. 'What a band.'

I nod, even though the band that sing it on the playlist is called the Bobby Fuller Four.

'I didn't think you'd be home,' I say, sheepishly.

Dad grabs a can of Coke from the fridge and cracks it open. 'Took a half day,' he says. 'Not that anyone cares at that place. I could show up dressed like a baboon and they wouldn't notice. You want one?'

I nod and he passes me a can. I'm gasping with thirst after the ride and the sweet coldness feels good slipping down my throat.

'So I've been doing some digging around your man's dad,' says Dad, sitting down and motioning for me to do the same.

I pull out the kitchen chair and sit down, dropping my bag on the floor.

'What have you found?' I ask

Dad sticks his tongue out. 'Not much. I found a Colin Longley in Belford, but he no longer lives at that address and no one knows where he's gone. It's as if he's disappeared.'

My stomach constricts like it's being twisted by a giant. 'You don't think he's dead, do you?'

'No,' says Dad, but he elongates the word so it almost sounds like a question. 'I'm pretty sure he's still alive. Eighty per cent sure.'

I'm not sure I like the sound of that.

'Look, don't worry, he'll turn up,' says Dad. 'Anyway, about this blockade thing.'

I close my eyes. I've been expecting this chat.

'I'm happy for you to go along with it,' he says. 'To a point. But I don't want you getting arrested, OK?'

'Agreed,' I say. I've seen films about prison and they don't look much fun.

'Good,' he says. 'And for my part, I'll try and keep your mother sweet.'

'Thanks, Dad,' I say.

He holds up his hands. 'I can't promise anything, though. Just be sensible and it will be fine.'

As soon as he says it, the door swings open and Abi walks in. 'We now have a hundred people committed to joining us at the blockade!' she says, without so much as a hello. 'We are going to take down the Establishment!'

Dad looks at Abi, then back at me. 'Remember how the song goes, kids. I fought the law and the law won.'

The Henry Branch Show, Radio 2

They asked me to go on, but when they said they have an audience of three million people, I remembered I had something more important on and sent Abi instead. She was more than happy to fill in.

HENRY: That was REO Speedwagon. Wow, what a band. Thanks to everyone who called in for our last talking point: 'Trees: are they a waste of time?' Some very strong arguments on both sides. But now, we move on to something a little different. The unremarkable Bedfordshire town, Pondstead, is poised for a showdown outside a disused homeless shelter. In May, the residents of Pondstead church hall were informed that they would have to vacate the premises due to funding cuts, which they did, only to illegally return and set up home there soon after. The council have warned them again to leave, giving them a deadline of this Friday, but local action group, the Soup Movement have announced they will blockade the site and prevent the removal. In the studio, I have Roger Swinford, leader of Pondstead Council.

ROGER: Good afternoon, Henry.

HENRY: And on the line I have Abi Turner, better known by her online pseudonym, Abi xx, one of the co-founders of the so-called Soup Movement.

ABI: What do you mean, 'so-called?'

HENRY *(after an uncomfortable silence):* It's just a figure of speech.

ABI: Pretty belittling figure of speech, no? How would you like it if I called you 'the so-called broadcaster Henry Branch?'

HENRY *(fake laughter):* OK, I can see this is going to be a feisty exchange. So, we'll start with you, Roger. Throwing a load of homeless people out in the streets, that can't be right, can it?

ROGER: I'm quite disappointed that the argument has been framed in such simplistic terms. We are not 'throwing people out on the streets', we are simply reclaiming an asset that belongs to the council and the taxpayers of our borough—

ABI: That is so typical. You're only worthwhile if you make enough money to pay taxes; everyone else can take a running jump.

HENRY: Please, Abi, you'll get your turn. Go on, Roger.

ROGER: As I was going to say before I was so rudely interrupted, we will not be throwing these people out on the streets. There are other shelters and charities in the area—

ABI: That are at breaking point as it is. You can dress it up however you like, but people are going to be on the streets with nowhere to go.

ROGER: I'm sorry, Henry, but it's impossible to have a civilized debate with someone as belligerent as this.

ABI: Belligerent? If you think I'm belligerent now,

just wait and see how I am at the blockade on Friday. No Dad, I will not calm down.

ROGER: Be as belligerent as you like, sweetheart, it won't make any difference when the police are taking you away.

ABI: Sweetheart? SWEETHEART? You patronizing old—

Abi's mic is turned down.

HENRY: OK, thanks very much, Abi. We'll be right back after this from Cliff Richard.

CHAPTER

28

It's the day of the blockade. Six in the morning, to be precise. I can't remember the last time I was up this early. Probably when I was in hospital and sleep was always as thin as spider-spun silk. My nightmares were off the charts last night. I dreamed of enormous bats swooping on the blockade and carrying people up into the night sky.

I stand in front of the mirror and splash my face with cold water.

Look at you, says my stupid brain. *You're supposed to go out there and lead a protest? You're pathetic! And that zit on your chin? People are going to think it's an extra head and start feeding it soup.*

I close my eyes and count to ten. Maybe I can't do it. I mean, who's going to listen to me?

The door rattles. 'Hurry it up in there. Some of us have to look livestream ready.'

I feel a little bit of weight lift from my shoulders. At least I won't be alone. And Abi has no problem telling people what to do.

I was hoping that Mum would still be in bed, but no such luck. When we get up, she's sitting at the kitchen table, mug of coffee in hand.

'Ohhh,' Abi moans under her breath.

'Promise me one thing,' Mum says, not even bothering with a 'good morning'.

'OK,' I say.

'You stay out of trouble,' she says. 'I understand why you're doing it. I actually agree with you. But I can't have you getting hurt.'

Abi goes over to Mum and gives her a hug. 'It'll be a peaceful protest, Mum,' she says. 'No one is getting hurt.'

Dad gives us a lift to the hall. It's pretty quiet at the moment. I see Gus sitting on the steps outside with a couple of others, but that's it.

'All the best,' says Dad. 'If you need me, give me a call. Stay safe.'

Abi salutes him.

Dad goes to drive off, then stops. 'Do me a favour, kids,' he says. 'Wish me luck, as well.'

Me and Abi look at each other. 'What for?' I ask.

Dad winks. 'Never mind what for. Just wish it.' And with that, he drives away.

'What do you think that was all about?' I ask Abi.

'Not a clue,' she says, as we watch the car disappear down the street, past the industrial units. 'Parents are weird.'

We sit next to Gus and wait for everyone to arrive, and they do, in dribs and drabs. First Harry, then Elaine, the Captain and Daniela.

'I feel like we're in the trenches, waiting to go over the top,' says Gus. 'Bet you know what that's like, Harry.'

Harry sniffs. 'Well, we weren't in the trenches, but I know what it's like being under siege.'

'Oh yeah?' says Gus.

'Yeah,' says Harry. 'Me and a few other lads were on patrol. Routine stuff, you know. Me and my old mate Beefy go into this abandoned building to check it out when outside, all these four-by-fours pull up, and we're surrounded.'

I gulp. I know what happened to Beefy, but he doesn't know that I know.

'We had nowhere to go. There was no way we'd stand a chance if we went out. I radioed for backup but for all we knew it would be too late. We had to hide in this room, behind a crate. Backup arrived just as they were getting to us.'

Harry stopped and took a shaky breath. 'Sorry.'

'It's alright,' I say. 'You don't have to talk about it.'

Harry shakes his head quickly. 'No. I should talk more. Need to get in the habit, you know?'

Before anyone can speak, an acoustic guitar chord from halfway down the street makes us all look up. Sure enough, there is Mr Grimshaw, in a pair of ripped jeans and a 'Make Love Not War' T-shirt, striding towards us, guitar in hand. He'd arranged for me to have an authorized day off school to be here.

'The stuffed shirts that run the school board won't like it, but this protest will be a real education for you, and if that's not what school's about, I don't know what is,' he told me.

He'd been fired up by the coverage the protest had got over the week. Roger Swinford was all over the place, calling Abi and me lawbreakers and promising to clamp down on us. The Prime Minister was even asked for comment and came down on the side of the council. It had caused a debate across the whole country, with everyone picking a side. One of the national newspapers ran a story, claiming that some of the hall's residents were criminals who couldn't be trusted. This was all because a couple of them had arrests for shoplifting on their records, which they had only done because they were desperate. I tried to avoid it, but Abi kept up with every update, putting out statements against the things the press were printing and filming angry livestreams, urging people to come down and join the blockade.

Mr Grimshaw sniffs the air and beams a contented grin. 'Looks like the perfect day for a happening. Any of you cats been to a protest before?'

Gus and the others say no. He knows that Abi and I have, so that goes without saying.

'I used to hate protestors,' says Harry. 'When they demonstrated against the war, it felt like a slap in the face to me and my brothers. Looking back, they were right.'

I see a load of cars parking up down the road. It's getting busy now. I knew it would, but there was always that voice at the back of my head, telling me that no one was going to show.

Daniela sits cross-legged on the floor, sketching

the scene. Some people have brought placards. Quite a few have snacks and drinks. Mr Grimshaw has started playing songs on his guitar and people are singing along. I'm not, because I've never heard of any of them. There's a friendly atmosphere, but with a tense edge. No one knows when the council are going to arrive.

By now, there's a line three people thick across the front of the church hall, with more arriving by the minute. There must be a hundred here now. Some people look like the kinds you'd find at protests, but others don't. It's like loads of people have realized how unfair this is. And like Elaine says, yeah, life is unfair, but that doesn't mean we can't fight it.

A brief burst of a police siren cuts through Mr Grimshaw's ragged strumming, and two cars turn into the street, escorting a council van.

Abi squeezes my arm. 'Here we go.'

'Yep,' I reply. 'Here we go.'

THE HOSPITAL BLOG

I've been back in hospital for three days now and Rio has hardly spoken to me. She just lies there, earphones in, frowning at her tablet. Every now and then, she'll grunt in frustration and throw it down on the bed. I asked her yesterday what she was doing, but she just said, 'Working.'

We can't go to the rec room like we used to. She has to stay in bed all the time. I asked Kate what was wrong with her, but she just gave me one of those thin smiles and said, 'Things are taking it out of her, darling.'

Me too. I thought treatment should be easier this time around because I'm used to it, but it really isn't. I spent all day yesterday staring at the ceiling and concentrating really hard on not puking. At some point, I remember hearing my phone beep but I couldn't bring myself to open my eyes. By the time I was well enough to look, it was about four hours later. It was from Rio and it just said, 'Remember to breathe, Ollie.'

I turned my head to look at her, but her bed was empty. To begin with, I thought she'd just gone to the toilet, but half an hour passed and she didn't come back. Then an hour. Now it's been three. Where is she?

CHAPTER
29

I recognize Roger Swinford, leader of the council, straight away. I've seen so many photos of him over the past few days, I could probably tell you how many hairs he has sprouting out of his left nostril.

He's a big frog of a man, with lips that turn downwards at the edges, and wide, expressionless eyes. When he stands opposite us, hands on hips, the entire crew erupts into a chorus of boos. He smiles a little, then opens a hold-all and pulls out a megaphone.

Abi rolls her eyes. 'Of course he has one of those.'

'This is Pondstead Council,' he honks. 'We are asking you politely to disperse immediately.'

No one moves. Roger runs a hand down his face. 'OK, have it your way.'

One of the police car doors open and a policeman gets out. Roger goes up to him and whispers something in his ear.

'Come on,' says Abi. 'We're going over there.'

She grabs my hand and drags me.

Roger grumbles under his breath when he sees us.

Abi blanks him, focusing instead on the policeman. 'We know our rights,' she says. 'And we are exercising our right to peaceful protest.'

The policeman, who, I can see from his badge, is called PC Nash, nods in agreement. 'I know. We're just here to make sure there's no aggro.'

Roger throws the megaphone back into the hold-all. 'So you're telling me all we can do is stand here and wait for them to go away?'

PC Nash, who I can tell thinks Roger is an idiot, calmly smiles. 'We can't go up there and drag them all away, I'm afraid. Like the young lady says, they have rights. We're all going to have to be patient.'

'Fine.' Roger pulls a flask, much like the ones I use for soup, out of his bag. 'I'll wait as long as it takes.'

He disappears back to his car for a second before reappearing with one of those fold-up chairs you might take on a fishing trip. He puts it down next to the police cars and plonks himself there, looking like a narked-off toad.

'This is it,' says Abi, pointing her phone at Roger.

'The face of oppression.'

'How do you sleep at night?' Someone at the back yells.

'Very well, thank you,' Roger replies, pulling a newspaper out of his bag.

Two vans pull up to the end of the street, and I can tell what they are from the huge satellite dishes on top.

'Oh, God, the TV is here,' I say.

The doors open and teams of technical-looking people get out, lugging cameras and microphones, followed by sleek, blow-dried reporters in snappy suits. It quickly becomes clear that this is two rival crews that have arrived at the same time. I wonder if they're going to have a scrap?

I recognize the reporter from the first van. You usually see her doing reports about turnip-growing competitions and things like that. The other guy looks kind of familiar, but I don't think I know him. His greying hair is slicked back and he's looking around like he's scared he'll catch something. I move a little closer so that I can listen to their conversation and figure out what they're planning.

'Hi Tony,' says the lady, a little frostily.

The bloke nods. 'Hannah, was it?'

'Rachel,' she says. 'I worked with you for three years, remember?'

Tony chuckles a little. 'Of course. So you drew the short straw, eh?'

'I wouldn't say that,' says Rachel. 'This is a big story.'

'Not exactly a snap election, is it?' he says, scoffing. 'Anyway, let's get this show on the road and get out of here as quickly as we can.'

His attitude is familiar. It's the same as Ross's was when he visited. Like this place is somehow less-than because it's not a big city. I start feeling defensive, which is about when I realize that I actually consider this place my home now. Pondstead. A place I hadn't even heard of a year ago.

'Excuse me?'

'Huh?' I'm snapped out of my daydream by a voice. It's a young lad with a pair of headphones around his neck.

'Are you Jordan?'

'Um, yes.'

He sighs as if he's relieved. 'Great. Could we grab a quick word with you?'

'A word?' I say, confused.

'Great!' He shoots me a thumbs up as if I've just

agreed to it. 'Mr Brassard, I've got him!'

That Tony bloke appears next to me like a vampire. 'So you're the Soup Movement kid, are you?'

A cameraman gets into position in front of me and another bloke holding a big furry mic stands next to him.

'No!' I squeak. 'Well, yes I am, but I don't do the talking. My sister, Abi does all of that.'

'I know,' says Tony, 'but it looks like those amateurs on the other side have beaten us to it. He nods over at Abi, who is already talking to the reporter and gesticulating wildly.

While I try to protest, the lad with the headphones hands Tony a mic and says, 'And we're live in five, four, three, two . . .'

'Live?' I shriek. 'What do you mean, "live"?'

Tony subtly elbows me in the ribs with a smarmy smile on his face. 'Thank you, Anita. Yes, I'm here outside Pondstead Church Hall where protestors have formed a blockade to prevent the council from removing its residents. With me now, I have Jordan Turner, who started the Soup Movement pressure group behind today's protest. Jordan, what are you trying to achieve today?'

I stare at the black hole of the camera lens and my brain whirs. I imagine all the TVs tuned to my face right now. I see the TV in our lounge at home, with Mum sitting in front of it, shovelling mints into her mouth. I see TVs all over the country being watched by the kinds of people who say we should be made to do national service and that we have no respect for the rule of law. I see the little monitors suspended on arms above hospital beds, being watched by kids like me. And Rio.

'Jordan?'

My mouth moves, but nothing will come out. The lad with the headphones is gesturing at me, his face slack with horror. There's a hand on my shoulder. My brain somehow gets the signal to my neck to turn my head and I see Harry standing there.

'Hold on a second, who are you?' Tony asks, irritably.

'My name's Harry. I'm one of the people Jordan has helped.'

Tony looks to Headphones Man for guidance and he seems to gesture for him to continue.

'And do you live in the centre?'

'Nah,' says Harry. 'I prefer my own company so I live in a tent. Besides, I'm sometimes a bit, you know, difficult at night, so it's best for me not to be around others.'

Ah, now it makes sense. He's probably living in the tent because he's embarrassed of his nightmares.

'And what is your view on what the council is doing here?'

'Nothing surprises me any more,' says Harry. 'When you're homeless, they don't care about you. You're just a nuisance. See this?' He bends down and unclips his prosthetic, holding it up to the camera.

'Oh, good Lord,' Tony whispers.

'I got my leg blown off for this country and how does it repay me? I'm left out on the streets, living in a tent.' He brandishes the leg at the camera like it's an accusation. 'And it comes to something when kids are having to make soup to help people out because the government won't do it.'

'Well, what do you say to people who say that you should stand on your own two feet?' says Tony.

Both me and Harry raise our eyebrows at Tony and he splutters, 'Pardon the expression.'

I know what I want to say. I want to say that people don't realize that it could so easily happen to them. They just have to fall in love with the wrong person, or become ill, or . . . or there are hundreds of reasons. No one sets out to be homeless, but like Elaine says, 'life ain't fair.' That's what I want to say. But I can't get the words out.

'What do I say to those people?' says Harry. 'I say—'

I'll stop there. The words he comes out with are not suitable for broadcast and Headphones Man looks like he's going to collapse.

The cameraman turns to focus only on Tony, who splutters an apology and clicks at Headphones Man, who ushers us as far away as possible.

'Thanks for that,' he says, his voice dripping with sarcasm.

'Serves you right for press-ganging the boy into an interview he didn't want to give,' says Harry. 'Now leave him alone, you bunch of parasites.'

'Charming.' Headphones Man shakes his head and walks away.

I look at Harry standing silhouetted against the sun and see past what he is now to the brave man that marched into a war zone, believing his country was behind him.

'Thanks, mate,' I say. 'You saved me back there.'

'It was the least I could do,' he says, reattaching his leg. 'No one messes with my little bro and gets away with it.'

He stands back up and flashes me a proud smile. I smile back. Harry surrounds himself with all these layers to keep the outside world away, that when he peels them back, even for a second, it's special. Hmm. Who does that remind me of?

Another police car pulls up and an older man gets out. He looks more senior than the others. Roger stands up and goes over to him. I can't hear what he's saying over all the chatting and Mr Grimshaw's dodgy singing, but I can tell he's agitated.

'What do you reckon his problem is?' says Harry.

'I don't know, but I doubt it's good news,' I say.

The older cop says a few words, then gets back in the car and drives away. Roger, with a satisfied smile, picks his megaphone back up.

'I have just spoken to the chief of police,' he says, through squeals of feedback. 'And he has informed me that this protest legally has to end at midnight tonight. Anyone obstructing council business after that will be removed by police.'

The assembled protestors boo him and a sandwich narrowly misses his head.

'Hey!' Elaine wriggles her way out of the crowd

and stands in front of them. 'No more throwing stuff. If we do that, we give them an excuse to crack down on us before midnight, and we are showing these cameras that we're as bad as they make us out to be. So behave.'

Harry applauds. 'Well said, Elaine.'

Fresh from her press tour, Abi comes over. 'Did you hear that? The midnight thing?'

'Yes!' I say. 'What are we going to do?'

'We stay put,' she says. 'We see it through to the bitter end.'

'But we promised Mum and Dad we wouldn't get arrested,' I say.

Abi laughs. 'Would Gandhi have worried about what his mum and dad said?'

'Um, probably not,' I say, unsure exactly what Gandhi got up to back in the day.

HONK HONK!

I turn around and see Maxwell slowly pedalling a bike up the road, flanked by Imran and Daria. He's pulling a trailer with two huge silver soup urns on.

'Lunchtime!' he yells.

He pulls up in front of the crowd and Daria gets some styrofoam cups out of her bag. It's only now that I see what they've done to the trailer. It has 'The

Soup Movement' painted on both sides in graffiti style. It looks so cool.

'This is brilliant,' I say, going over.

'Right?' says Maxwell. 'Old Grimshaw got us out of lessons to make soup all day. Beats Maths, know what I mean?'

'Less of the old, young man,' says Grimshaw, tuning up his guitar.

'And I did the trailer,' says Daria. 'Thought you could use some branding.'

I feel bad about letting Will get into my head about them. They're not doing this for fame. They're doing it because, like me, they've realized it feels good to help people and to feel like you're making a difference. Mr Grimshaw watches on proudly as they dish out steaming bowls to the residents.

'This is a special moment,' he says. 'Real people power. Right, who's up for singing some Joan Baez?'

'Maybe later, mate,' says Gus.

I walk away and try to take it all in. I don't know what's going to happen, so I'm trying to stay in the moment and not freak. The reporters have retreated to their vans for the time being and things have become less tense. The best thing is seeing people who've come for the protest chatting and laughing

254

with the residents. It's like we've removed that invisible barrier between homeless people and the rest of the world, if only for a day. If the people here will stop and chat with them after today, then no matter what happens to the hall, at least we'll have made a small difference.

I take a little stroll down the street to stretch my legs and get a change of scenery. The police are leaning against their cars, talking amongst themselves as new people arrive to join the protest, probably after having seen it on the news. Maybe Harry's swearing was what drew them in. Every little helps.

I approach the corner where me and Harry crashed into that postman when I nearly bump into someone coming the other way.

'What are you doing here?' I say to Will.

'We need to talk,' he says.

A REAL SCRAPPER

I first started to panic when I noticed her stuff was gone.

'When did that happen?' I asked Dad.

Dad looked up from his work phone. 'When did what happen?'

'Rio's stuff,' I said. Her books, her snacks, her tablet were all missing.

Dad lifted his glasses onto his forehead and squinted over at Rio's bed. 'Oh, some nurses bagged it up and took it out while you were asleep.'

I sat up too fast and was hit by a tsunami of nausea. I took five deep breaths and tried to visualize blue flowing into red. 'Did they say where they were taking it?' I rasped.

'No,' he said. 'Probably wouldn't tell me if I asked. Confidentiality and all that. Anyway, you get some rest.'

'I need the toilet,' I said, swinging my legs out of bed.

'Do you need help?'

I shook my head and struggled to my feet, before making my way up the corridor towards the nurses' station, but it was like being on a ship in the middle of a storm, with the floor seeming to tilt upwards. Kate emerged from a side room pushing the medicine trolley. When she saw me, she gave me a smile which didn't reach her eyes.

'What are you doing out of bed, Jordan?'

I tried to speak, but I was so exhausted, I couldn't get the words out.

'Hold on a sec.' She wheeled the trolley back where she got it from, then slowly led me to the rec room. There was a kid from a different area in there, playing a game on an iPad.

'Sorry, Ismael, could you give us a minute?' said Kate, plonking me down on the sofa.

Ismael shrugged, got up and made for the door.

'Thank you, my love,' Kate called after him.

I stared at the blank TV and tried to remember to breathe while Kate sat next to me.

'I suppose you want to know where Rio is,' said Kate.

I nodded and managed to rasp out a 'Yes'.

Kate shifted her position to get a better look at me.

Up close, I noticed her eyebrows were drawn on. The other day, Rio told me she was 'back on the dating scene and making an effort again.'

'So I don't know if you're aware, but Rio's prognosis got worse over the past month,' she began. 'She wasn't responding to treatment the way we would have liked.'

'OK,' I said, finding my voice. 'So why not try something else?'

Kate smiled again. 'Everything that can be tried has been, sweetheart.'

I shook my head to try and clear it. 'So where has she gone?'

'Intensive Care,' said Kate. She went to say something, then stopped herself and put her hand on my shoulder. 'It looks like she doesn't have much longer.'

If chemo feels like being hit by a car, hearing that felt like being crushed by a train. I kept thinking I was having a really bad dream, and I'd wake up, screaming and embarrassed, with Rio laughing at me from the next bed. But it wasn't. It was real.

'I want to see her,' I said.

Kate sighed. 'We're not supposed to, but . . . If your parents agree, you can go up for a little while.'

Dad agreed. I wasn't going to let him not. When Kate had finished the meds round, she put me in a

wheelchair and took me up to Intensive Care with
Dad. The lights were dim up there. It was quiet. It was
the opposite of our ward.

Kate stopped outside a room, left us outside and
went in. After a few seconds, she came back out and
wheeled me in. Dad waited outside.

Rio's mum and dad and Simone were all sat around
the bed. They looked exhausted. Rio was hooked up to
breathing tubes. How could things change so quickly?
She didn't look brilliant this morning, but at least she
could breathe by herself.

Rio's mum gave me a whispered, 'Hi, love,' and
stood up so I could take the seat closest to the bed. I
didn't know what to say. She didn't look like she could
hear me, anyway. I touched her hand. It felt warm but
as fragile as a precious vase.

'Love you,' I whispered. It was the only thing I could
say that even came close to what I felt. And I do. I do
love her.

When Kate wheeled me back out, Simone followed
and asked if she could have a word with me. Kate
pushed me into a little waiting room and left the two
of us alone.

Simone sat opposite me and gave me a thin smile.
Her eyes were puffy and her hair was beginning to

grow back.

'I'm glad you came to see her, Jordan,' she said. 'She would appreciate that.'

I wiped a tear from my cheek. 'She'd probably tell me to stop being such a wimp.'

Simone laughed lightly. 'Yeah, she probably would.' She stopped and shook her head. 'I just can't believe it's happening now. We knew the day would come eventually, deep down, but . . .' She trailed off and looked at the ceiling.

'She might pull through,' I said, my voice quivering. 'I mean, you never know.'

Simone nodded. 'Maybe. She's done it before. This time seems different, though. I can't explain it.'

I noticed Kate look in through the window. I could tell she wanted me to go back to bed pretty soon.

'When Rio was six, we were told she only had two more years,' said Simone. 'She's a real scrapper, that one.'

I had no idea. She never told me she was terminal. For a second, I felt something close to anger, but I quickly pushed it away. She didn't have to tell me anything. But maybe it explains why she dreamt up this mitzvah thing. She wanted to leave something behind.

CHAPTER
30

I look around, checking to see if this is some kind of ambush. The old kneel-behind-you-and-push-you-over trick. That would bring me back down to Earth. Literally. But there's no one there and Will looks serious. More serious than I've ever seen him.

'Are you sure this is a good idea?' I say. 'Why don't you just go home?'

He blinks hard. 'No,' he says, firmly. 'It's important. Can we just sit down for a minute?' He gestures at the kerb. Checking he hasn't somehow booby trapped it or something like that, I take a seat and he follows.

Looking at Will properly for the first time since he arrived, I notice the dark rings under his eyes and his fingernails chewed to nubs.

'I've been thinking about what you said,' he starts, his voice cracked and barely audible above the sounds of the protest.

'About what?'

'Cancer,' he says.

'What is it?' I say. 'You need more proof? Well, I'll see if I can get you a copy of my medical records, yeah?'

The voice in my head that always tells me to be nice starts piping up and I know it's right, but I just don't trust him.

'No,' he says, running a hand over his face. 'No, I believe you.' He stops and swallows. 'I've got something to tell you.'

'What?' I ask, expecting him to drop the act and say something about being glad I was sick. That's exactly the kind of trick he'd pull.

'My mum had it.' He blurts it out quick, like it's one long word.

I study his face for some sign that this is a sick joke, his sickest yet, but there's none.

'She had all this chemotherapy and it's gone now,' he goes on. 'But I'm scared that one day it'll come back and I'm . . .' He tries to catch his breath and his eyes go slick with tears. 'I'm just so scared.'

With that, he gives up trying to hold back the tears and dissolves into a series of racking sobs.

That voice kicks in and tells me what to do. I put my arm around him and rub his back. Sometimes that's all you need. I know that. As I let him cry it out, I start to realize some things about him. That this is the reason why he acts the way he does. That the only thing he feels like he has control of is his friendship group, and when they tried to parachute me in, he freaked out. He probably felt like a boat with its mooring-rope snipped, drifting away from everything.

Will has stopped crying, but his breath is still jerky and he's struggling to get his words out. 'I just want you to know . . . that I'm sorry for how I've been acting. It's . . . it's because . . .'

'Because of your mum,' I say. 'I get it. I know what it's like.'

Will dries his face with his sleeve and takes a breath. 'It feels good to talk to someone about it,' he says.

'So you haven't before?' I ask.

He shakes his head. 'No. The school knows, but that's it. I haven't even told Max and all of them. You probably think that's weird.'

'No,' I say. 'I haven't told them about what I've been through, either, remember? It's because I don't want people to think I'm different, or to pity me. I bet it's the same for you, right?'

Will seems to think about it for a second, then nods.

'And I deal with it by throwing myself into the Soup Movement thing, whereas you do it by putting on a front and trying to make people think you're invincible. I don't want to blow my own trumpet, but I reckon my way is better.' I stand up. 'Come on. Join us.'

His eyes go massive. 'But I can't. I'm the one that reported them!'

'All the more reason to make it up to them,' I say. 'And anyway, they don't know it was you. You might not want to let too many people hear your voice, though.'

'Why?'

'No reason.'

'Hey, it's Will!' Max yells as he doles soup into a cup. 'He's come over from the dark side!'

The others cheer him as he takes a ladle and starts helping. I catch Mr Grimshaw's eye and he looks as proud as if Will was his own child.

I hope this is a new start for him. I hope his Mum

will be OK.

I need some time to myself. It's exhausting being around so many people. I'm just looking for a quiet corner when Abi jumps in front of me with a planet-sized grin on her face.

'Everything alright?'

'Course it is!' she yells, grabbing me in a bear hug. 'We're getting traction, my friend. *Traction.*'

'What are you on about?'

She's says nothing else, just pulls her phone out of her pocket and shows me some of the top trending topics in the country. Number three is #AddPootoaFilm. Number two is #PondsteadProtest. And number one is #Harry.

'Wow,' I whisper.

Abi nods excitedly and clicks on #Harry. Instantly, the screen is flooded with tweets from people saying how much they love Harry. Stuff like 'Tell 'em Harry! #hero.' And it looks like a close-up of Tony's face at the exact moment Harry swore is on its way to becoming a meme.

'See what I mean?' says Abi. 'Traction!'

Sure enough, new people are arriving all the time. Some of them are lining up for selfies with Harry.

'Look at you,' says Elaine. 'You're like a rock star.'

'Rock n roll!' the Captain yells.

I take a seat on the steps outside the hall and glance at Roger. He looks even more miserable than he did this morning, if that's even possible.

When school finishes, a few kids from our year show up to be part of the protest, as well as kids I don't even recognize that must have come from other schools.

After his fiftieth selfie, Harry makes his excuses and comes over to me. 'I'm going to head inside for a bit,' he says, pointing at the hall. I don't blame him. It's all a bit much.

Some of the kids from school have brought a ball and start a game of dodgeball. At one point, the ball knocks over Roger's flask and he gets on the megaphone saying that, 'Any further acts of aggression will result in arrests.' The police officers roll their eyes at each other.

The sun is beginning to go down behind the industrial units, casting an orange light over everything.

'Nice evening for it.' I look up and an old man is standing over me, smiling. He's dressed in a brown suit with a green, flowery tie and his white hair is slicked back.

'Are you the boy I saw on television earlier?' he asks.

My face flushes. 'I guess so. I didn't say much, I know.'

The old man laughs. 'You did fine. So, is he still about?'

'Who?' I ask, confused.

'Harry.'

'I think he's having a lie down. All the attention has worn him out a bit.'

The old man nods. 'Well, do you think you could let him know I'm here whenever he's ready?'

'Um, OK,' I say. 'What's your name?'

'It's Colin.'

CHAPTER
31

I open the main door to the hall and walk inside. It's empty, except for Harry, who is sitting with his back against the wall, his knees drawn up under his chin. He's looking straight ahead, but it's as if he's not really there. His eyes are blank and faraway, like his brain has floated out of his head.

Colin follows behind me and I hear a sharp intake of breath when he sees Harry in the flesh for the first time.

'Harry?' I say.

He doesn't respond, still stuck in his trance. I lean forward and gently shake him. Some recognition comes back to his eyes.

'Alright, mate?' I say.

He nods. 'Little bro.'

'You've got a visitor.' I take a step to the side and let them look at each other properly. Harry stares, like he's trying to figure out if this is real or not, then his face crumples and he buries his head between his knees.

Colin goes over and slowly sits next to him, pulling him in for a hug. 'It's alright, son,' I hear Colin whisper. 'I'm here. I'm here.'

I decide to give them some privacy and come back outside. Colin must have seen Harry on TV. I try and imagine what it must be like not to see your son for years, only to have him turn up on the news, homeless.

They stay in there for the rest of the night. Every now and then, I step in and take them a cup of tea each from the van that has set up in the street, and it looks like they're catching up.

See that? says the voice in my head. *Isn't that a mitzvah?*

At some point during the evening, Mum has shown up. I don't know how long she's been there, but I can see her car at the end of the street. I wave at her, but she doesn't get out. She's here to keep an eye on us, I bet.

It's getting dark now and I'm dog tired. Roger isn't giving up, though.

'The time is now eleven thirty pm. You have

thirty minutes to disperse.'

Then, as if to underline his point, two police riot vans pull up.

'Here we go,' says Gus. 'We're going over the top.'

Marlon, standing next to him, cracks his knuckles. I've got a bad feeling about that.

The doors of the riot vans open and four armed officers get out. I see Roger smirking through the gloom. Every one of them has a baton on their belt.

'Here comes the oppression,' says Abi. 'Down with the police state!'

As the clock ticks closer to midnight, the police start to get ready, standing in a line and staring us down. The singing and chanting has stopped and the only sound is the hum of the tea van's generator.

My heart pounds and I feel my chest rising and falling too fast. Without thinking about it too much, I take out my phone and scroll to a message I must have looked at a hundred times.

Remember to breathe, Ollie.

It's good to have a reminder.

I see a shape hurrying up the street and soon it's level with the police. 'Jordan, Abi, come on now,' it says.

'Not now,' Abi groans, 'we're live-streaming.'

'I don't care,' says Mum. 'Home. Now.'

The news cameras are fixed on us and I wish for some kind of power cut to stop them filming this.

'Nope,' says Abi, folding her arms.

'I am your mother and I say you're leaving now. Don't make me come over there.'

'Good idea,' I say.

Mum glares at me. 'What?'

'I said good idea. Come over here and be part of it.'

Mum gawps as the entire assembled crowd cheers and applauds. She shakes her head. 'No. No I'm not.' But the crowd starts chanting, 'Mum, Mum, Mum, Mum!' Eventually, she walks over.

'The two of you are so grounded after this,' she says, through a fake smile. 'You have no idea how grounded you are.'

The door behind us opens and Harry and Colin step out. They stand next to us, their arms around each other.

'Everything OK?' I ask.

Harry gives me a thumbs up on his dad's shoulder. Colin nods at the riot cops. 'Things have taken a turn since we've been inside. What's going on?'

'We've got,' Abi checks her watch, 'fifteen minutes to leave before they move in.'

'But it won't come to that,' says Mum. 'We're leaving now.'

'We're not,' Abi whispers to me.

'I never thought I'd see you at a protest, Harry,' says Colin.

Harry chuckles. 'Me neither.'

Mr Grimshaw moves over to Max, Will, Imran, and Daria. 'Right, hep cats, I think I need to get you out of the way in case things go south.'

'No way,' says Will, pouting defiantly. 'We're staying until the end.'

Mr Grimshaw rubs his forehead. 'I wish I'd sent out permission slips.'

Roger worms his way in front of the police with his megaphone. 'Five minutes,' he says.

I notice some people on the edges slipping away, losing their nerve. I can't blame them. I want to run, too. It's only that voice in my head that keeps my feet planted to the floor.

'Bring it on,' says Marlon, crackling with menace.

I hear a car pulling up behind the police and a door opening and slamming shut. I can't quite make out the identity of the figure that's running towards us. Mum beats me to it.

'Graham?! What are you doing?'

'Stop,' he says, holding his hands up.

'Who are you?' says Roger, through his megaphone.

Dad looks at us and gives us a thin smile. His hair is frizzed out from his head and his tie is so loose it's more like a scarf.

'I am Graham Turner,' he says. 'And I have the paperwork in my briefcase, which, when I sign it, will make me the owner of these premises.'

A gasp goes through the crowd. Mum leaps forward like she's spring loaded. 'Graham! What are you talking about?'

Dad sighs. 'Claire, Kellmans offered me my redundancy today, and I accepted it.'

'Oh,' says Mum.

'I've been there for over twenty years, so they're giving me a good payout. A really good one,' he says. 'And I've decided I'm going to use it to move into the catering industry.'

'What are you talking about?' says Mum.

Dad turns and points at the church hall. 'You're looking at the world's first Soup Movement restaurant,' he says.

'Restaurant?' says Mum. 'You can't open a restaurant for homeless people. How will you make money?'

Dad shakes his head. 'It's not going to be for homeless people. Not like that. I'm going to employ them. If they're up for it, that is?'

The hall residents cheer.

'That's a relief,' says Dad.

Mum's head whips from Dad, to us, then back to him. 'But how? What about all the, you know, paperwork?'

Dad sticks his hand out. 'Hi, I'm Graham. Your husband. Accountant for twenty-five years. Pleased to meet you.'

Abi taps me on the shoulder. 'What's happening?'

'I'm not sure,' I reply.

Dad takes Mum's hands in his. 'I've been festering in a miserable job for too long. With selling the old house and now this redundancy payout, we've got plenty of money. It's time for an adventure.'

Roger stomps over to them. 'It's midnight!' he booms. 'Officers, disperse these troublemakers!'

Dad doesn't even look at him. He just opens his briefcase, takes out some papers and signs them.

'As of now, this property is mine. Now clear

off, or I'll get the police to escort you away for trespassing.'

Roger turns purple as the protestors erupt into the biggest cheer of the day. All around, people are filled with joy. Abi holds her arms out. 'How about it, little brother?' she yells over the noise.

I shudder exaggeratedly. 'If we must.'

Abi rolls her eyes and pulls me in tight. Maybe she's alright, really.

UNTITLED

'She's gone.' That's what Simone's text said.

I wanted to get out of bed and go up to intensive care, but Mum wouldn't let me. She had to pin me to the bed and I was too weak to put up much of a fight.

I don't know what I would have done if I'd got up there. I guess I just needed proof that it was true.

It doesn't make sense. How can someone like Rio, someone so full of energy, someone so funny, someone so . . . *her* just not be around anymore?

It's been three days now. This is the first time I've been well enough to write. And I got another message from Simone. It said, 'Before Rio passed, she made me promise to send you this. For what it's worth, I know she spent ages on it because of the amount of times she messaged me for advice!'

I clicked the link and it took me to a Spotify

playlist, compiled by 'Riooooooooooooo.' It was titled, 'Ollie'. It's twenty songs long and I haven't heard of any of them, but I pressed play on the first one, closed my eyes and listened. It was incredible. Like every song was written about us. Some of the songs were sad, some funny, some angry, but it flowed like they belonged together.

It wasn't until track six that I remembered something. What Rio said the first time we met.

'I only make playlists for people I love.'

Oh, Rio.

CHAPTER
32

When the reminder flashes up on my phone, it takes my breath away: *Meet Rio to discuss Year of Mitzvahs.*

I'd never got around to deleting it. Probably because I didn't want to. Doing that would be admitting that it couldn't happen.

It's been two weeks since the protest outside the church hall and things have been moving fast. Dad has assembled a team, including Gus and Marlon, to help gut and refurbish it. The back of the building is being kept as a shelter, but most of it is going to be the Soup Movement Restaurant. He's aiming to open in a month.

There's a knock at my door. Ugh. It's seven o'clock on a Sunday morning. Unless the house is literally on fire, there is no need to be knocking my door at this time.

'What's up?'

The door opens and Mum sticks her head inside. 'Wakey wakey, let's be having you.'

I rub the sleep from my eyes. 'Have we started going to church or something?'

'No, but we are going for a day out,' says Mum, who I've just noticed has rollers in her hair. 'Back to the city.'

I sit up. 'What for?'

'It's a surprise,' she says, tapping the side of her nose. 'I've hung your outfit on the back of the door.'

'Outfit?' I say, but she's gone.

I don't like the sound of that. I lie in bed for another minute before finally dragging myself up. I unzip the bag to find a three-piece black tuxedo suit, complete with bow tie. What's going on?

I run downstairs and find Mum and Dad in the kitchen. Dad has had a shave and seems to have finally cleaned two weeks of refurb dust off himself.

'Why am I wearing a tuxedo?' I ask. 'Where are we going?'

'The zoo,' says Dad. 'We've got you a spot in the penguin enclosure.'

Mum playfully smacks Dad's arm. They've been getting on a lot better these past couple of weeks, probably because Dad is so much happier.

'Don't listen to him, Jordan,' says Mum. 'It's a surprise!'

'Why can't you just tell me?' I moan, stamping my foot like a toddler.

'It'll be brilliant, trust us,' says Dad. 'We're just not allowed to tell you what it is. Strict orders. Now hurry up and get ready. We leave in precisely one hour.'

In a daze, I head back upstairs. I stop by Abi's room on the way. She's putting mascara on in the mirror.

'Do you know what all this is about?' I ask.

She doesn't answer right away because for some reason it's impossible to talk and apply mascara at the same time.

'Yes,' she says. 'But I can't tell you what it is.'

'Why not?' I ask.

'Because, little brother, sometimes surprises are nice,' she says. 'And besides, if we told you, you'd freak.'

I beg her to spill, but she pushes me out of the room and snicks the lock that she installed herself.

I don't need this today. I just want to sit and think about Rio and our pinky swear. The others probably don't realize. Why would they?

I put on the suit and look at my reflection in the bathroom mirror. What could this surprise possibly be? Some kind of fancy party? Since when do we get invited to fancy parties? Abi says I'll freak if I find out, but I'm freaking right now.

When I get downstairs, Mum, Dad and Abi are waiting for me, all dressed up. Abi tuts, and fixes my hair, rubbing some kind of wax into it.

'So handsome,' says Mum, her eyes twinkling.

'He's going to be fighting them off with a stick,' says Dad

'Fighting who off with a stick?' I moan, on the verge of a full-blown tantrum.

Dad checks his watch. 'Never mind that, we've got to go.'

We all pile into the car while my brain whirs like a centrifuge trying to work out where we're going. It's clear nothing is going to get them to tell me. My threats to jump out of the car are met by Dad activating the child lock and saying, 'Checkmate.'

I concentrate on the scenery whizzing by: the countryside giving way to the concrete of Pondstead, giving way to the motorway, nearly empty this early on a Sunday morning.

Abi snaps a selfie with me in the background

before uploading it to Instagram with a caption saying 'ON OUR WAY!'

'To where?' I moan for what must be the fiftieth time.

Abi squeezes my cheek. 'You'll find out soon enough. Now sit up straight or you'll wrinkle your tux.'

'I promise you it's nothing to worry about,' Mum says from the front. 'It's exciting, that's all.'

Don't believe her, Jordan, says my stupid brain. *She's trying to lull you into a false sense of security. You need to worry. Worry like crazy. DO NOTHING BUT WORRY.*

Sounds like a plan.

We get off the motorway and head into the city centre.

'I don't miss this trip,' says Dad. 'There's something to be said for living five minutes from work.'

He swings the car into a multi-storey car park and finds his reserved spot. We get out and everyone grins at each other, all wide-eyed and excited.

'OK, we're here now,' I say. 'So will someone PLEASE tell me what's happening?'

'All in good time,' says Abi. 'All in good time.'

I follow them out of the car park and I notice lots of signs stuck to pillars: AKA THIS WAY. What does that mean? We walk a little way along the street until we arrive outside the National Arts Theatre. We drove past it on the way in and Dad whistled appreciatively at it, as if he'd never seen it before.

'Ta-da!' says Abi, spreading her arms like she's made it appear out of a top hat.

I look up at the building: a grand dome with ancient figures in poses under the roof. And that's when I see the sign.

Amazing Kids Awards: Celebrating our Finest Young People.

'Why have you brought me to watch this?' I ask.

They don't answer, just grin at me. My stomach twists. I feel sick.

'This is my surprise?' I say.

Dad shoots me a double thumbs up. 'Winner winner, chicken dinner!'

My mouth drops open. I can't speak. Mum puts her arm around me.

'It's no problem,' she says. 'You just have to go on stage and accept an award.'

'What award?' I manage to rasp.

'Best Charitable Contribution,' says Abi. 'The organizers emailed me a few weeks ago to let me know you'd won.'

'AND YOU DIDN'T TELL ME?'

'As I explained earlier, you'd freak,' says Abi. 'And you had enough on your plate with the church hall and everything else.'

'Nothing to it, son,' says Dad. 'You just go up there, say a few words and get off.'

'SAY A FEW WORDS?'

Dad winces. 'Yeah. Don't worry, they won't be expecting anything Oscar-worthy.'

'I've got you covered,' says Abi, pressing a piece of paper into my hand. 'Just read that and you can't go wrong. I haven't even gone on about your amazing, beautiful sister that much.'

I feel numb as they lead me inside. We're met by a lady in a smart suit and with a headset mic on.

'Hello, Jordan,' she beams. 'I'm India.'

'Wow,' Dad whispers, with fake awe. 'Two countries meeting. It's like the UN.'

Mum smacks Dad's arm. 'Sorry about him. We're all very excited to be here.'

India laughs. 'Dad jokes are an occupational hazard at events like these.' She hands us a guest pass each and gets another staff member to usher Mum, Dad and Abi to a lounge. Wishing me luck, they left.

'OK,' says India, still smiling. 'Let's show you where you'll receive your award.'

I follow her along the corridor, trying to regulate my breathing. This is no big deal. It's probably going to be in some side room; the kind of place you'd hold a birthday party with a disco. There'll be like fifty people there, and they'll only be families of award winners. It's basically a school play.

India holds her pass up to a panel and leads me through a set of double doors into a dark room. I follow her past some workers hunched over electrical equipment and suddenly, I'm blinded by an intense light.

'OK Dave, that's fine, you can cut it now.' I hear a staticky voice from a walkie-talkie and the light goes.

It takes a second for my eyes to adjust, but when they do, I let out a little yelp.

'So here we are,' says India, gesturing out at THE ACTUAL NATIONAL ARTS THEATRE. THE MAIN ROOM YOU SEE ON TV.

There are seats sloping way up near the ceiling in an enormous horseshoe shape. Everywhere I look, there's seats.

'Will this be full?' a squeaky voice that I guess is mine asks.

'It should be,' India replies. 'About five-thousand people.'

FIVE.

THOUSAND.

Pretty big school play, eh Jordan?

I notice a big mechanical arm suspended above the auditorium. It starts moving slowly, backwards and forwards. I decide to concentrate on that and try and forget about the five thousand people that will soon fill every available space and stare at me.

'What's that?' I ask India.

'Oh, that's for the sweeping crowd shots,' she says. 'There'll be other cameras for what's happening onstage.'

I clear my throat and try to sound casual. 'Cameras, you say?'

India laughs. 'Of course! The Amazing Kids Awards are televised every year.'

I take in what she's saying. I really absorb it. Abi was right when she said I'd freak. The only thing she didn't count on was me freaking when I got there.

'Are you feeling OK?' India asks me, probably

noticing that I look like I'm going to faint.

'Fine,' I lie. 'I could just do with a glass of water.'

'Of course,' she says. 'We'll go through to the green room now.'

She leads me off the stage, back along the corridor and into a room about the size of our school canteen, but a lot posher. There are dozens of tables and at the back of the room there's a huge buffet. Not that I could even attempt to eat right now. We sit down at a table and India brings me an ice-cold glass of water, which I down in one.

'Wow, you really were thirsty,' she says

I nod, but the water hasn't helped. It's like trying to put a forest fire out with a Supersoaker.

'Actually, India, where is the nearest toilet?' I ask, climbing shakily to my feet.

'Just over there,' she says, pointing at the huge signs. 'Are you going to be alright?'

I nod and make my way over there. When I'm inside, I splash my face with cold water and look at my reflection.

Let's get real for a second, says my brain. *You can't do this, can you?*

'No,' I say out loud.

So why don't you be sensible and make a quick escape?

Just go and sit somewhere quiet for a few hours; they'll give the trophy to Abi in your absence, and then you can all go home to Pondstead where it's nice and calm. That sound like a plan?

'Yes,' I say.

Of course it does, it says, flooding me with feel-good warmth. *Now let's go.*

GOODBYE TO STARGIRL

I'm in trouble. Worth it, though.

Simone messaged the other day with details about Rio's funeral. I said I'd be there. How could I not be? But I didn't reckon with Mum. She said I had to stay in hospital for treatment, and being in a place with so many people would be bad for my health, not to mention how upsetting it will be.

I tried everything. I refused to speak to her, I refused to eat. Even Kate had a friendly word with her and said an hour or so out of hospital won't be a problem. She wouldn't hear it, though. Appealing to Dad did nothing, either. I get the feeling if it was up to him, he'd have let me go, but it very much is not up to him.

We had just had another one of these arguments and Mum and Dad went off for a drink, leaving just me and Abi. She didn't say anything and stared at her phone. I had to ask her what she thought. She put her own and looked at me.

'I think, yet again, the woman is being totally unreasonable. Did you know she won't allow me to go to Morocco for a creativity retreat? It's like living under Stalin.'

'I need to go, Abi,' I said. 'I never got to say goodbye to her properly.'

Abi sighed and looked out of the window. 'Maybe there's something I can do. Maybe there isn't. Bear with.' And with that, she went back to her phone.

So that's how I ended up crouching in the back of Leonard's BMW in my pyjamas this morning. Abi turned up early, all dressed in black. She was supposed to be in college so this was double the potential nightmare for her. She threw my coat at me. 'Right, come on. Quick.'

We headed for the door as fast as we could. As we passed the nurses' station, Abi yelled a cheery, 'Just taking my little bro out for some fresh air!' at Pravina, before mashing the green door release button and leading the way into the corridor.

Downstairs, the sleek, black car was idling in the pick-up point. Abi got into the passenger side and I got in the back.

'Greetings, adventurer,' Leonard boomed from the driver's seat.

'Um, hello.'

'You may have known me as Leonard before, but all my brothers and sisters in arms call me Dragon.'

'They do not,' Abi snapped. 'Not once have I heard someone call you that. Right, hurry up before we get caught.'

'Very good, fair maiden,' he said, putting it into gear with a clunk that would have awoken someone in a coma on the eighth floor.

As we pulled away, Abi threw a plastic bag full of clothes at me. 'Here's your outfit.'

'Am I supposed to get changed back here?' I asked, horrified.

'No, Jordan,' she replied, flatly. 'We're going to nip home so you can freshen up.'

'But I can't get undressed in front of you!'

Even though I couldn't see her face, I could tell Abi was rolling her eyes. 'Maybe I won't look. Maybe the thought of my little brother's body isn't as exciting as you think it is.'

'Yes, you must armour up, young warrior,' said Leonard/Dragon. 'Don't fret. As an experienced lord of the shire, there is little mine eyes have yet to witness.'

Abi tutted. 'Why are you talking like that?'

'Why?' he replied, in that same voice. 'For we are on an adventure! Tis only right! There will be foes to slay, mead to sup and damsels to save.' When he said that last bit, he waggled his eyebrows at her, to which she groaned and said, 'In your dreams, Dragon Boy.'

I pulled the suit out of the bag and laid it on the seat. If I was methodical about it, I wouldn't have to sit there just in my pants. I pulled off my pyjama top, then put on the shirt, then I did the trousers, before finishing off with the jacket and tie.

Soon, we arrived at the church and parked a little way up the road. I saw the hearse pulled up outside and I thought I was going to be sick. She can't be in there. She just can't be. Abi turned around. 'You OK?'

I shook my head.

'If it's too much, you don't have to go in,' she said.

I opened the door before I could be talked out of it. When my feet hit the floor and I stood up, I noticed the problem with my suit. And so did Abi.

'Ooh, ankle swingers.'

Of course. It had been about eighteen months since I wore that thing. You could completely see my Iron Man socks.

'Look, don't worry, that's actually very in right now,'

said Abi, but I could tell she was struggling to keep a straight face.

Leaving Leonard in the car, Abi and I headed into the church. It was packed and we had to stand at the back. As soon as we did, a bloke saw me and insisted I had his seat. He practically threw me in there.

I took the briefest of glimpses at Rio's coffin as it was carried in. It looked so small. Too tiny to contain someone like her. I closed my eyes and tried to remember to breathe. There were speakers set up and a song started to play. It took me a few seconds, but I recognized it as one of the songs from the playlist she made me. The next thing I knew, Abi was shoving a tissue under my face. I didn't know how long I'd been crying.

I can't look at Rio's parents. How can they cope? I know they knew this day would come eventually, but . . . It's just not fair.

A vicar stood at the front and started yammering on about God and I just wanted to scream. Hey God! If you're so great, why did you let this happen? Why create someone as incredible as Rio and torture her with illness all her tiny life? Why did you give me leukaemia? I direct these questions silently skyward, but no answers come back.

The vicar introduces Simone to the front. She's wearing bright green trousers, a billowing red blouse, and a big pink hat.

'Rio made me promise I'd wear this,' she said. She laughed a little, then took a quick breath. 'Rio was my little sister and she was my best friend. But she was more than that. She was far more wise than I will ever be. She taught me about the world, about life. She taught me that, if there's any point to all this, it's to be kind and to help people.' Simone stepped back from the microphone, touched her fingers to her lips, then gently rested them on the lid of the coffin.

Just then, music came out of the speakers. It took me a few seconds but I soon recognized it. Stargirl. Simone sang beautifully. I had no idea how she could do it.

You are my stargirl,
Forever by my side.
Shining bright through the blackest
of nights.

'Rio was a beam of light,' Simone continued after the song was over. 'And as long as her goodness and kindness ripple out into the world, that light will never go out.'

That was when I realized; it's up to me to keep her light burning. I promised to carry on what we started and there's no way I can back down. She wouldn't forgive me.

I left before the burial. I couldn't bring myself to see that. When we arrived back at the hospital, Mum was waiting outside, her arms folded and her mouth full of mints.

'What do you two think you're doing?' she barked.

Leonard wound the window down. 'Greetings, fair maiden! We have returned from our crusade!'

Mum's eyes went huge as she stared at me, then at Abi, then back at me. 'Get out of that idiot's car right now.'

I went back to bed, trying to screen out Mum's constant carping on about 'betraying her trust'. There's someone new in Rio's bed now. Life goes on. Mum was going off on one at Abi about how disappointed she was, when I felt Rio's light within me and knew exactly how to stop her.

'Mum,' I said.

'What is it, Jordan?' she snapped back.

'I love you,' I said.

It worked. Thanks Rio.

CHAPTER 33

It must be meant to be. There's a family heading
into the ward and I'm able to ghost in behind them
when they're buzzed in. They look at me a bit weird,
probably because a tuxedo isn't obvious hospital
wear, but I don't make eye contact and use them as a
shield from the nurses' station.

I find the rec room empty and close the door
behind me quietly. Nothing has changed in here.
Even the books are the same. I sit down on the
battered old sofa and scooch down so I won't be seen
if anyone looks through the glass in the door.

As I close my eyes, the memories come flooding
in like I'm a boat with a hole in the bottom. *A
Midsummer Night's Dream*. The busker. Our first
kiss. So many nights spent together on this sofa, just
chatting and laughing. The kind of stuff that seemed
so small and unimportant at the time but now looms

in my mind as huge and as intense as the midday sun.

I take a deep breath. Then another. Then another. I really am calmer here. I can hide out the day where I am, no problem. I feel myself sinking deeper and deeper, my heart rate slowing. I am truly relaxed.

'Nice threads, Ollie.'

AARGH! The voice comes from nowhere. I sit up with a jolt and look around. There, sitting on the sofa next to me is Rio. She looks different. For one thing her skin is glowing. Not like she looks heathy, but I mean literally glowing. And she has hair like she did on that photo at her funeral. Funeral. FUNERAL.

'H-how are you here?' I manage to stammer.

'Relax,' she waves me off casually. 'That's not for you to know.'

I want to get up and run away, take off down the corridor screaming 'GHOST!' But I can't. I can't move.

'So what's this I hear about you skipping out on the awards thing?' she says.

I shake my head. 'I can't do it.'

Rio laughs. I've missed that laugh. As precious and hard as a diamond. 'What, you can't accept a nice prize and have a load of famous people tell you how incredible you are? The struggle is real, bro.'

'You know what I mean,' I say. 'I'm not supposed to be up there alone.'

'You won't be,' says Rio. 'The bloke from that gardening show will be there with you.'

I choke out a weak laugh. 'I mean you should be with me.'

Rio reaches across and grabs my hand, making it glow like hers. 'We both know that's not going to happen,' she says.

My face is wet. Those tears are back. The ones that come with no warning.

'I know what your problem is,' says Rio, gently. 'You feel guilty because you survived and I didn't. You feel like something has gone wrong and one day the Big Man is going to realize his mistake. That about cover it?'

I nod, my breath going jerky.

For a split second, Rio disappears before exploding back into vision, her face centimetres from mine. 'Listen,' she says. 'You've got to stop thinking like that. There's no reason for this stuff, OK? No grand plan. Stuff just happens. But you don't waste this. You don't waste a single second. You get out there and you live and you soak up every last drop of it, do you understand me?'

I'm sobbing now and I can't talk.

'There's a whole world out there to explore,' she says. 'You're going to listen to music. You're going to fall in love. You're going to get married. If you want to, that is. You're going to hug a cute puppy. You're going to laugh. Oh, mate, are you going to laugh. You're going to make friends. Real ones. Just as soon as you open that cast iron shell of yours and let people in. Those nightmares will stop eventually. Quicker if you get help. You're going to be so happy one day that you're going to stare at the sky and allow yourself to wonder if it wasn't all made for you.' She leans in and kisses me, softly, tenderly. 'You're going to have a ball, Ollie.'

I fight to regain control over my lungs. I never want this to end. I want to stay in this rec room with her forever.

'Well you can't,' says Rio.

'Wait, can you read my mind?'

'Here's what you're going to do when we're finished,' she says. 'You are going to leave this hospital and run as fast as you can to that hall. You are going to accept that award. You are going to allow yourself to bask in the glow of the crowd.

Then, and I can't stress how important this is, afterwards, you are going to visit me.'

'What, here?'

'No, not here, dumbo,' she flicks my forehead. 'You're going to visit where I'm buried.'

I gulp. 'But I don't want to.'

'Why?' she asks, seeming a little offended.

I sigh. 'Because, because.'

Rio shakes her head impatiently. 'Because you don't want to think of me as being gone, right?'

I think about it for a second, grasping for some other reason, but she's right, so I nod.

'And that's precisely why you need to go,' says Rio. 'And there's another reason, too.'

'What's that?'

Rio makes a 'my lips are sealed' gesture. 'I can't say. But it's very important, so you have to promise me you'll be there.'

'OK,' I say. 'I promise.'

Rio smiles. 'Alright. I've got to go.'

'Wait, Rio, please don't go!' I cry.

'I have to,' she says, fading further until I can barely see her. 'And so do you.'

I try to grab her hand, but it's gone. She's gone.

CHAPTER 34

When I run back into the hall, India has turned grey.

'Jordan! Where have you been?' she cries.

'I'm sorry,' I say. 'I had to go and see a friend.'

She clasps her lips together and nods. 'OK, well a word of warning would have been nice.'

I'd already texted Abi to let her know I was on the way back. She replied with a load of question marks. I'll explain later, I'd said.

We go back to the green room and this time India has backup—a huge security guard called Clyde. We sit at the table and watch the show start on a big TV. I can feel the rumble of the crowd vibrating through the building. But I'm not scared. Talking to Rio, if that's what really happened, has calmed me right down. I feel like I can do anything.

India nods at me. 'Are you ready? We're up next.'

'Ready,' I say.

She clearly doesn't believe me because she gets Clyde to follow behind us, but soon we're right behind the curtain. I can hear the orchestra playing through the break.

A bloke with an earpiece in jogs over to us. 'This the soup kid?' he says to India.

'Yes, this is Jordan,' says India.

'Well, glad to see you're no longer AWOL,' he says. 'Just as well. If the Amazing Kids Awards lost a kid, it'd be terrible publicity. Right, when Anton says your name, you go on, shake his hand, take the trophy and say a few words. You've got a minute. Minute-and-a-half tops. If you see a red light flashing, get off. Any questions?'

I shake my head.

'Alright, break a leg.'

The orchestra reaches its big ending and the host, a lady from that dancing show whose name I've forgotten, goes up to introduce Anton. I can see him a little way down. Mum is a big fan of his. He presents a gardening show and always goes on about how we should sing to flowers. He's probably a bit mad.

I hear Anton talking about the Soup Movement. I catch the odd phrase: 'courageous young man', 'worldwide phenomenon', but it's like he's talking about someone else.

India squeezes my shoulder. 'You'll be great,' she says.

I don't doubt it. Rio told me I would be. And she wouldn't lie.

'Jordan Turner!'

Earpiece man gives me a thumbs up and ushers me through a gap in the curtain. I see Anton clapping wildly and grinning at me like his face is going to split in two. I hear the roar of the crowd, even though all I can see from the lip of the stage is a yawning black chasm. Anton hands me a trophy and guides me to the microphone, where he gestures for the crowd to cheer louder, and they obey him like they're a giant flowerbed he's crooning to.

I fumble in my pocket for the piece of paper Abi gave me earlier, but it's not there. I check my other one just in case. Empty. It must have fallen out somewhere. Here goes nothing.

'Thank you,' I say, my voice booming back at me through the speakers. Wow, do I really sound like that? 'This has been a huge surprise for me. I didn't find out what was happening until I got here because my family reckoned I'd freak if I knew in advance.'

The audience laughs, a big, warm wave washing over me.

'I couldn't have done this without the help of a lot of people,' I say. 'First of all, my sister Abi. She spread the Soup Movement all over the world, and if she didn't like to fight so much, we wouldn't have stood up to Safebuys and Pondstead Council.'

The crowd applauds. I bet wherever Abi is in that inky blackness, she's loving it.

'And I should thank my Mum and Dad. It was Mum that started making soup in the first place. She just didn't know what I was doing with it.'

More laughter. I have to stop for a second. Normally, I'd be thrown by that and get flustered, but my stupid brain isn't talking rubbish to me. It hasn't been since I spoke to Rio.

'And Dad got sick of his job and has started running the Soup Movement restaurant, so I should probably thank his work for being super depressing, too.'

While the crowd laugh again and applaud lightly, I shield my eyes from the light so I can see them. Wow. So that's what five thousand people look like. I drop my hand again before I lose my nerve.

'I'd like to thank Harry Longley for all his help,

as well as Elaine, Daniela, the Captain, Gus and all the guys from the shelter.'

Another round of applause. The light is flashing. I'd better get off.

'One last thing,' I say. 'None of this would have happened without one person. We pinky swore exactly a year ago that we would do as many good things for people as possible and see how much the world has changed. Well, Rio.' I stop, and listen to her name echoing around the hall. 'I reckon it's changed a fair bit. I love you. Bye.'

And with that, I take my trophy and leave the stage, the applause and cheering booming around my head.

After the ceremony, there's photos and interviews and Mum has her picture taken with Anton, who tells her she should be very proud. Abi digs me in the ribs.

'You were incredible up there!' she says. 'In front of all those people on your own.'

'But I wasn't on my own,' I say.

'Well, I know the gardening man was up there, but.'

'No, I don't mean him,' I say. 'It was Rio. She was with me.'

Abi smiles, and her eyes brim. 'Oh God, Jordan, I'm going to have to reapply my mascara.'

I find Dad in a corner, talking to a retired footballer, and I tell him I want to leave.

Dad rolls his eyes. 'Alright.' He turns to the footballer. 'I don't know, these kids moan when I move them out to the suburbs, but now they can't wait to go back.'

'No, I don't want to go home,' I say. 'I want to go and see Rio.'

Dad says goodbye to the footballer and walks me away, his hand on my back. 'Are you sure that's a good idea?'

'I don't know,' I reply. 'But I have to go, I've been told.'

Dad looks confused. 'By who?'

I think about it for a second. I could tell him, but he'd probably think I'd gone completely cuckoo. 'Doesn't matter,' I say. 'So can we go?'

'I can't exactly turn down an Amazing Kid now, can I?' he says, with a grin. 'I'll go and fetch your mother before she leaves me for that bloke that tap-dances at rosebushes.'

When Dad comes back with Mum, we get back in the car and make our way to the cemetery. I've never been there before. I've never wanted to. To be honest, I still don't. Dad parks the car in a bay near the entrance and turns around.

'Do you want us to come with you, or would you rather fly solo?' he asks.

'I'll go alone,' I say.

I start walking up the hill, past row after row of old headstones, until I find the newer ones. I know Rio's when I see it in the distance. I don't know how, I just do. I'm drawn to it.

They did Rio proud with her stone. It's brilliant white marble, and someone has hung a pair of headphones on top of it. Next to her name is an oval portrait, the same one they used at her funeral, the one with that big smile that bursts with life. I dry my eyes with the cuff of my tuxedo.

'Did you hear my speech?' I ask. 'I mentioned you.'

I stop and wait as if I'm expecting her to answer. She's not going to. And it doesn't look like she's visiting like she did in the rec room. If she did. I could have fallen asleep and had a really vivid dream. I suppose I'll never know for sure.

'Anyway,' I say. 'We promised each other a year

ago that we'd meet up today and see how the mitzvah thing has changed things. So, here I am, holding up my end of the bargain.'

I extend my little finger and touch it to Rio's hand on the portrait. 'I'll come back on this day every year,' I say. 'I'll get my grandkids to give me a lift when I'm a shambling old geezer.'

I stop because the sadness of it all makes my breath catch in my throat.

'Pinky swear,' I say, moving my finger up and down.

'Jordan? Is that you?'

I jump so high, I nearly take out a weeping angel three rows down. When I turn around, my hand clamped over my chest as if to keep my heart from bursting through my ribs, I see Simone standing there, holding a bunch of flowers.

When she can see that it definitely is me, she runs over and wraps me up in an enormous hug. I close my eyes and bask in her warmth. When she releases me, she stands back and looks at me like I'm an expensive work of art. 'You look so good!' she says, that big smile on her face. 'So healthy!'

I've never been good with compliments, so all I can do is shuffle from foot to foot. 'I mean, I've seen you all over the Internet with your Soup Movement thing, but seeing you in the flesh is different.'

She shakes her head. 'That reminds me, I've been meaning to get in touch with you. I started my own chapter at uni.'

'That's brilliant,' I say.

Simone puts the flowers in front of Rio's grave, then kisses her fingertips and presses them to the stone.

'It's nothing,' she says. 'I feel like I'm continuing her work in a weird way, do you know what I mean?'

'I know exactly what you mean,' I reply.

Simone looks at me, thoughtfully, like she's trying to work something out. 'So how come you're here today?'

I shift again, unable to look at her. 'I was in town for this awards thing, and—'

'So you didn't dream about her?'

My eyes snap to hers. 'I don't know,' I say. 'I'm not sure what happened. Why? Did you?'

She nods. 'Last night. She told me to come here at five. She said it was important. And I told her, it's kind of awkward, because we're having this big family party and . . .' She trails off. For a second, she looks confused, but then this look of total understanding crosses her face.

'Oh, Rio,' she whispers, smiling. 'You're still twisting us around your little finger.'

'What do you mean?'

'Have you got an hour to spare?' she asks. 'I need you to meet someone. Rio needs you to meet someone.'

CHAPTER
35

I got Dad to follow Simone back to their house.
There are lots of cars parked outside. This must be a
big party.

We find a space, and make our way inside. Mum,
Dad, and Abi don't know why we're coming, but I've
used my status as an Amazing Kid to insist that we
do.

Simone leads us through the crowds of people,
all standing around, nibbling food from paper
plates, until we reach the conservatory. There's a
little girl sitting in a chair, playing with a doll. She's
probably about four. She has tight, curly brown hair
and the biggest eyes I've ever seen. She looks like a
Disney character. Simone kneels in front of her, and
speaks to her gently.

'Hello Elsie,' she says. 'I'm so sorry to bother
you again, but I've brought a friend with me and he

wants to hear the gift Rio gave you.'

Hear the gift? What does that mean? Simone looks at a lady sitting in the chair next to her, who I'm guessing is her mum. 'Jordan and Rio were really close. Is it OK?'

'Of course,' says Elsie's mum. 'I'm always listening to it, myself.'

What are they talking about? Is it some kind of playlist? Since when do four-year-olds care about playlists?

Elsie's mum reaches into her bag and pulls out a stethoscope, before handing it to Simone. Wait. A stethoscope? Why does she need that? Oh.

'Sorry, darling,' says Simone. 'I know it's cold.'

She presses the pad of the stethoscope onto Elsie's chest, through a gap between the buttons of her dress, then motions for me to kneel beside her. I quickly turn to look at Mum, Dad, and Abi. Mum has her hand clamped over her mouth and her eyes are filled with tears. Abi, who would normally be filming a moment like this, can only watch in amazement.

I place the buds into my ears and gasp.

Dum DUM, dum DUM, dum DUM.

A massive smile spreads across my face as I listen

to the same heart that started such an amazing thing, beating on in the chest of the little girl, giving her a second chance at life.

'Wow,' I whisper. 'This is the greatest mitzvah of all.'

EPiLOGUE

I thought that the nightmares would stop after I saw Rio, but they haven't. I guess when something is hardwired into your brain, you can't just switch it off. So I remembered what Rio said and I told Mum about it. She booked me in at the doctor's and even though it was all a bit embarrassing, I now have an appointment with a therapist in a few weeks. When I told the doctor all about it, she said it sounded like PTSD. Like Harry.

Speaking of Harry, I heard from him the other day. He went home with his dad after the protest and that was the last I knew. But today, the postman brought a parcel for me. I opened it to find a letter scrawled on some lined paper, along with a little plastic bag.

Alright, little bro?

Saw you on telly the other day. Nice one!
I just wanted to thank you for what you did.
It's proper amazing when you think about it.
I don't have much to give you in return, but I've sent you a little something. I don't want them myself, looking at them brings back the bad times. But you deserve them just as much as me.

Stay strong,
Harry.

I opened the plastic bag and two medals fell out. I couldn't believe he'd sent those. But I get why. I've pinned them to a board in my bedroom.

Harry isn't the only one who's gone away. Daniela had an offer to display her work in a big, famous gallery, and she sold most of her pieces and was such a hit she's been inundated with offers. She's renting her own flat now.

The Captain's found a place, too. There's a care home about ten miles away with a room that overlooks the canal. He's been there a few weeks and hasn't tried to escape yet, so it's going well.

It was the restaurant's grand opening today. Dad managed to get Anton the gardening man to come and cut the ribbon. Well, actually Mum did. We had queues down the street coming to sample our delights, all based on Mum's recipes. We were so busy, Dad got me and Abi to help wait tables, while Gus, Marlon and loads of others boiled up big pots of every variety in the kitchen. Leonard even showed up and offered to work as a pot-washer. Dad agreed, much to Abi's disgust. Still though, it's a really nice place. People seem to like it. You're welcome, too. Just walk in and our maître d' Elaine will greet you with her trademark catchphrase,

'Welcome to The Soup Movement. It's more than just soup.'

ABOUT THE AUTHOR

As well as writing books, Ben Davis has had a variety of jobs, including joke writer, library assistant, and postman. Writing books has proven the most fun.

Ben lives in Tamworth, Staffordshire, and in his spare time enjoys rock climbing, white-water rafting, and pretending to have adventurous hobbies.